£6

The ACROBATS of AGRA

Also by Robin Scott-Elliot

The Tzar's Curious Runaways

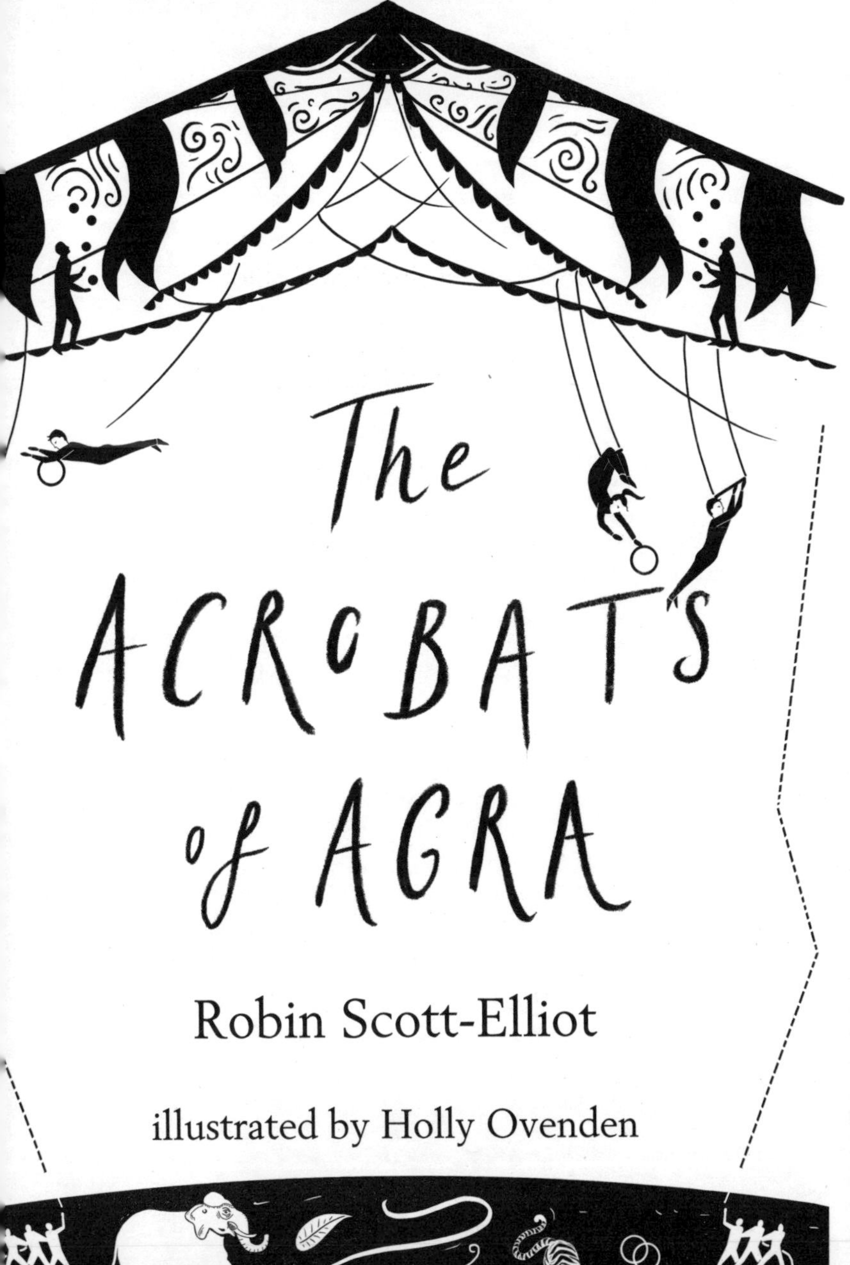

The Acrobats of Agra

Robin Scott-Elliot

illustrated by Holly Ovenden

Published in the UK by
Everything with Words Limited
3rd Floor, Descartes House,
8 Gate Street, London WC2A 3HP

www.everythingwithwords.com

A catalogue record of this book is available from the British Library.

ISBN 978–1–911427–14–8

Printed and bound in Great Britain by
CPI Group (UK) Ltd, Croydon CR0 4YY

To Torrin

"Prove to me you are the acrobats of Agra
& you will live."

1

The Great Romanini had a bird's eye view the night I pushed over general Biddle. I didn't mean to but that doesn't seem to count when it comes to knocking over generals. Especially ones as important as General Biddle.

His long row of medals, their ribbons all colours of the rainbow, tinkled like they'd caught a fit of the giggles as he tried to extract himself from Lady Stout's lap.

And all the time the Great Romanini flew above us and all the time I couldn't take my eyes off him. That's how it happened – because I tipped my head so far back watching the Great Romanini fly. I was spellbound, so spellbound and so tipped back I toppled over.

It was like a mini game of skittles. I fell backwards into General Biddle, who was only a wee man, and he tumbled into Lady Stout. There the game of skittles ended.

"Harrrummpphh," said the general.

"Well I never," remarked Lady Stout.

"Beatrice Spelling!" exclaimed Aunt Constance.

"Wow!" I said, listening to none of them.

How could I pay attention to anything but the mid-air magic trick being performed above our heads? I'd never seen anything like it and I'm pretty sure the city of Agra hadn't and, who knows, maybe even the whole of India.

"Roll up, roll up…" the ringmaster had cried as we squeezed sweatily into the makeshift stands beneath the large circus tent. "Come see the daring, the death-defying, the flying Frenchies… Romanini and Juliette."

I'd seen the red-and-white striped Big Top rise up on the plain outside the city two days before. Even the kite flyers hauled down their paper birds to watch. Posters appeared here, there and everywhere. I bubbled with excitement.

They made us wait to see the death-defiers. The main attraction always comes on last (otherwise everyone would go home as soon as they were done I suppose). It felt like a bit of forever. I'm not good at waiting, especially if I'm supposed to be sitting still. I'm a fidgeter you see. Can't help it, just the way I was born. But no one makes allowances for it. Wriggly Spelling is what Miss Goodenough, my teacher, called me on my first day in my new school.

"Miss Wriggly, sit still," she demanded and I tried and tried but no matter how hard you try, you don't always succeed.

I tried and tried in the Big Top as well; I sat pretty still during the first act, the fire-eater: a giant man with a shiny canon ball of a head who gobbled up flames as if he'd not eaten for a week. He was good but then the sitting-still test really began; through the horse show (loud and dusty), the magician (unconvincing), the world's strongest man (his claim), the bird lady (she sang and a row of green parrots sat on her outstretched arms and squawked along), the snake charmer (slithery) and the clowns (funny). Waiting, waiting. For the acrobats.

It's not that the others were bad – I laughed at the clowns because everyone laughs at clowns, even General Biddle and Lady Stout. It's just that it was the acrobats, and only the acrobats, I wanted to see. I could have happily sat and watched them for hours, WITHOUT MOVING A MUSCLE.

I admit I was getting wriggly when the jugglers, the last act before the acrobats, came into the ring and I could tell Aunt Constance, seated on my left, was getting cross. She dared not make a fuss because fussing wasn't done.

On my right, sitting ramrod straight and tight-lipped as ever, was Cousin Primrose. "Oh, do sit still,

Beatrice for goodness sake," hissed Primrose (she often hissed because those tight lips never seemed to open wide enough to let words out properly).

And then at long last there they were. My breath caught in my throat. The one and only, the flying wonders of the world, Romanini and Juliette – the ringmaster rolled the R at the start of his name and for good measure popped a handful on to the end of hers so it came out as "Julietterrrr".

I gulped down everything about them, every last detail. Each wore a white turban, but otherwise were dressed as if performing back home at the Cirque Napoleon in Paris – I'd seen drawings in the newspapers. Romanini wore a loose purple shirt with a large golden star on its back and front and skin-tight trousers tied above the knee. Juliette, her dark hair stacked on top of her head, wore a V-necked top in the same colours but with a golden lining and dark shorts also splashed with gold.

They ran holding hands into the ring in that confident, springy manner those at ease with their bodies seem to have. Not like me, according to Aunt Constance. She says I'm an awkward girl and tells everybody I have ten thumbs and I'm all elbows and sharp corners. I disagree. She doesn't know me. I disagree with Aunt Constance about lots. I don't try to; I just do.

Romanini and Juliette raised their hands, bowed and separated, moving with simple grace, bare feet skipping across the floor, and each leapt in one fluid motion on to ropes that hung on opposite sides of the ring. The Great Romanini was closest to me and pulled himself quickly up his rope to a swing, a thin wooden bar that hung from the roof of the Big Top.

Across the ring Juliette had done the same. I missed her climb – I decided to concentrate on Romanini because if you tried to watch both you ran the risk of seeing neither and that would be an absolute disaster.

Just below the two swings, a tight white rope stretched across the ring, tied between two of the great poles that kept the Big Top up. From down here the tightrope looked no wider than a single strand of a spider's web.

The small orchestra struck up as Romanini stood on the wooden bar and began to swing. Higher and higher he went until, all of a sudden, he let himself drop only to reach out and grab the bar in both hands as he fell.

"OOOOOHHH," said the crowd and me.

He swung again and this time when he let go he flew. That's what it looked like and that's why I fell back on to the general. The Great Romanini flew towards the tightrope.

"AAAAHHHH," said the crowd and me.

"Harrrummphhh," said the general, regaining his seat, his medals still tittering, his face as red as his uniform jacket.

My eyes remained fixed on Romanini as he threw out a hand and caught hold of the tightrope; his other hand missed its attempted grasp and he hung there for a moment or two, drawing another fearful gasp from the audience. Not from me – I didn't gasp because I had every confidence in Romanini. From the first time I saw a poster in the city I knew he would be remarkable. Of course, I had no idea then just how remarkable he would prove to be and how brave and how... wait, that's for later.

He swung himself again with just one hand, and wrapped his legs around the tightrope. In the blink of an eye he was standing upright, arms outstretched holding the pose and bringing a stutter of applause and some cheers from a group of red-coated soldiers clustered at the back of the stand.

There are always soldiers around Agra, but over the last few days more have arrived, marching and shouting here, there and everywhere, and there are more people too. The British settlement is getting ever so busy with families looking for places to stay. One woman arrived sitting on the front of a cart covered in dust, no hat, hair all over the place. I think she was crying. Good job Aunt Constance didn't see her – she would not have approved. Something's going on but that's for another day. Because right now there's only one show in town: the CIRCUS.

The Great Romanini bowed towards Juliette, who had swung on to a tiny wooden platform at her end of the tightrope. Her turn: she lifted her balancing pole and stepped on to the rope, a wobble, another "Ooohhh" from the crowd (and me) and then she steadied herself. She strode out towards Romanini and when she was near him she executed the perfect curtsey. I struggle to curtsey on solid ground let alone standing on a spider's web high above the earth. He bowed again.

Now they tried to pass each other and each waved a leg and arm as if they were on the brink of plunging back to earth.

They scratched their heads. Juliette raised her hand, as if an idea had sprung into her head. She made a series of gestures at Romanini and he nodded back. Juliette's legs started sliding in opposing directions along the tightrope and within moments there she was in the splits, pole held out to keep her balance, perfectly still, as though she were doing this on the front lawn.

"Allezzz hupppp," yelled Romanini, his voice carrying bright and breezy in the stifling heat of the Big Top. He took two careful steps back, sucked in a deep breath and leapt forward, a skip, a jump then he was airborne, twisting into a somersault and flying over Juliette, who remained absolutely, perfectly still. If I had been close enough I would have seen that the French girl did not even blink.

"Huuuuuaaahhhhh," I said and followed it with "Ooooohhhhhphew" as Romanini landed back on his feet, safely and securely, as only one of the world's greatest acrobats could.

I leapt to my feet.

"Watch out," said Lady Stout.

I clapped and clapped and clapped as loudly as I could until my palms stung.

The British soldiers joined in, jumping up and yelling their appreciation, as did the Pathans, tall and tough-looking men in turbans and loose robes with thick beards who come to Agra to sell horses to rich city folk. Sowars, Indian cavalry troopers in blue uniforms with extraordinary moustaches, stomped their booted feet on the wooden stands and whooped and hollered. A polite ripple of applause filtered through the rest of the British crowd.

"Beatrice Spelling, sit down in your seat at once," ordered Aunt Constance. Everyone, Aunt Constance was fond of pointing out, should know their place and stay in it. Primrose pulled at my arm. I brushed it off.

"Honestly, Beatrice, you are an absolute embarrassment."

"What will people think?" added Aunt Constance, glancing nervously behind her.

"Harrrummpphh," said the general.

"I am ever so sorry General Biddle – she's only just come out from home."

"Dogs, I tell you," muttered General Biddle, "England's gone to the damn dogs."

"I'm from Scotland," I said because I knew it would annoy Aunt Constance.

"Eh?" said the general, surprised a girl dared to even address him. Children were supposed to be rarely seen and NEVER heard.

"Shhh, Beatrice," commanded Aunt Constance, pulling me down hard into my seat.

It hurt, but only for a moment, because my eyes were already back in the heavens, which is what the top of the circus tent seemed to me. If only I could be up there with them: the Great Romanini, Juliette and Beatrice the Amazing Acrobat from Ardnamurchan. Maybe not Ardnamurchan – not many people in Great Britain let alone India have heard of the distant peninsula on the wild west coast where I grew up.

Tonight was the first moment I didn't wish I'd never been sent to India. You see, Mother and Father were sent here and look what happened to them. So I wasn't at all keen to follow, especially as it meant leaving Grannie.

I'd been taken from Grannie's only a few months

earlier after it was decided she was too old to look after me. I'd lived with her for six years, just the two of us, ever since Mother, Father and Baby George left for Father's new position…

I screeched. I wasn't sure whether it was the roars of the soldiers or the rush of air and thump of his feet landing on the ground that jerked me from my thoughts, but there HE was right in front of me, the Great Romanini, arms raised, acknowledging the applause for the grand finale of his act. And I'd missed it, missed seeing him fly off the far swing and hurtle through the air, swallow diving on to the rather unsafe-looking safety net.

He leapt up and danced across the net; Juliette copied him on the other side, before both somersaulted down to the ground, the orchestra blaring a triumphant conclusion.

"TAAA-DAAAAAH!"

"Bother," I said, drawing a hiss from Primrose, who was clapping her white-gloved hands so lightly she wouldn't have disturbed a fly.

I sat down. I was cross now. Only that morning, in the wake of another scolding from Miss Goodenough, I vowed I would pay more attention and stop disappearing into distant corners of my mind. I must stop my attention from darting here, there and everywhere like a monkey on a mad, mad mission.

"Bother, damn, bother, damn, bother damn and blast it," I said.

"Mother…" shrilled Primrose. I ignored her. I was staring at Romanini. Close up he was smaller than he seemed in the air but he looked strong. A lock of pitch black hair flopped over his forehead which he tried to blow away as he kept his arms outstretched to take the applause. It made him look younger than I'd supposed he was – in fact as I studied him I saw he wasn't much older than me.

A sudden movement behind him caught my attention. An animal slipped beneath the curtain separating the ring

from the backstage area. At first I thought it was a large cat. But as it raced across the ring towards Romanini, pursued by the fire-eater waving his colossal, shiny arms, I realised it was not the sort of cat I thought.

It was a tiger. And Romanini appeared to have no idea the beast was making straight for his back.

"Ohhhhh," I yelled and leapt once more from my seat, whirling my arms in alarm.

"Oooooffttttt," said General Biddle. Because this time I punched him – by accident and I really was so dreadfully sorry but still a punch and on the chin and I can punch quite hard. He fell back again, once more into the unwelcoming lap of Lady Stout. She shot up in alarm, surprising Mr Slasher, the city accountant standing with his back to the ring as he adjusted his hat in readiness to leave. Mr Slasher waved his arms in the air as if he were balancing on a tightrope but being no acrobat he failed to keep to his feet and toppled backwards on to Lady Stout, who in turn tumbled and buried general Biddle beneath her wide skirts.

"Harrrummpphhh-helllllllpppp," arose a muffled cry from the general.

I ignored it all because I had to save the Great Romanini. I hurdled the small fence separating our seats from the ring. Sometimes I just do things without thinking. I leap before I look.

I hurtled into Romanini, knocking him backwards. We tumbled to the ground just as the tiger arrived and leapt on top of us. Its breath was hot – and a wee bit stinky. I scrunched my eyes as tight shut as I could.

"Ahh, Tonton," said Romanini and when I opened my eyes again I saw the tiger licking Romanini's face. "Merci, mon ami, merci."

Hands grabbed me and pulled me to my feet.

"Damned disgrace," said a deep voice. It was Theophilus Campbell, the city's magistrate, one of the most important people in Agra. A typical snooty Campbell, Grannie liked to say of her son-in-law, Aunt Constance's husband… my uncle. "Absolute damned disgrace."

It was the most Uncle Theophilus had ever said to me. And it was the most furious I'd ever seen him.

"Oh dear," I said to no one in particular.

From my bed I could hear the cawing of crows and the chitter and chatter of sparrows and mynah birds outside the window. Beyond them came the squealing of kites circling the great and ancient city of Agra, riding the plumes of hot air rising from the baking earth.

The fan flapped above my head and I wished hard I was back home, wished I was anywhere but here. I'd been doing a lot of wishing recently.

"Pew, pew," I said in my most sing-songy voice, trying to drown out the sound of India.

"Pew, pew."

It was the sound of home, the call of the buzzard as it hunted above Glen Laddich where Grannie lived in a tumble-down draughty house at the end of a puddled drive. I closed my eyes, not too tight as that crushes the picture, and searched for the glen and the loch where I swam in water so cold it pick-pockets your breath.

I know every inch of the glen. I flew over it like a buzzard, hovering above my favourite places… I opened my eyes. It was not a pleasant daydream because it only reminded me how little I knew of India and the new life I was supposed to be having and not having at all.

"The time of your life," everyone said on the ship that sailed me out here. What did they know? I could see worry hidden behind their eyes. They didn't know where they were going any more than I did, and they were supposed to be the ones in charge.

I wonder if Mother and Father were anxious when they came out. A journey into the unknown. Grannie always said Mother was one of life's worriers. She'd been right to worry about coming to India. Not long after they arrived, sailing at last through the delta's brown waters to reach the busy port of Calcutta, fever gripped them tight.

I don't know exactly which disease or horrible

illness they caught because I'm only a child so don't get told anything. Except what to do.

But I do know what the fever did to them, my poor mother and father.

They died.

Baby George survived. After Mother and Father were buried, he was taken up country to Mother's other sister, the youngest, Aunt Celia. For better air, they said. That's where he is now. I haven't seen him since I arrived in India. I'm not sure he'll remember me. I barely remember him because it's been half my life since I saw him, or Mother and Father.

So we're orphans, me and George. That's what I am: Poor Orphan Beatrice. Aunt Constance's friends shake their heads and look sad when they see me. I don't want their sympathy. I don't want to be like them.

Back home, it took an age before me and Grannie found out what had happened; months of letters arriving in Scotland with dribs and drabs of news. By the time we were told the fever had carried them away they seemed long gone. They'd already left me once.

What I didn't see coming was what happened

to Grannie. She got old. That seemed much worse because it was before my own eyes. No mother should outlive her daughter, Grannie said, it's cruel. We cried together for a time, for her daughter and my mother – and I was crying for Grannie too. It was Grannie who brought me up. I feel comfort when I think of her hugging me. I can't feel Mother's hug. I have tried. I really have.

One day a cousin arrived in Glen Laddich, a bossy man with whiskers and a mousey face. He said Grannie couldn't look after me anymore and I was to go to India to live with Aunt Constance, Mother's eldest sister. Grannie cried again when I left. She tried to hide it but I could tell because I know Grannie. I cried too, in the mousey cousin's carriage, until he told me to pull myself together. Now Glen Laddich was a world away, an utterly different world to India.

Life here is governed by rules, rules and more rules, rules for everything: what you wear, how you speak, who you speak to, who you don't speak to, how you have your hair, what time you get up, what time you go to bed. The British are always telling somebody what to do. It never changes; from dawn till dusk you obey THE RULES.

It's like being tied up by invisible ropes. I hate it. I really do and I hate being shut in my room all Sunday as punishment for my "shaming and shameful unladylike behaviour" at the circus.

Soon lunch, like breakfast, will be brought to my room on a tray. At four o'clock the key will turn in the lock and I'll be let out to go to church, a punishment worse even than being locked in my room. Two hours squeezed between Aunt Constance and Primrose as the Reverend Potiphar mumbles and stumbles through a sermon, feeling the sweat trickling down my back in the dull heat of the church and getting a dig in the ribs from Primrose every time I wriggle.

Church has been extra crammed recently, so extra sweaty, because there are still more British families arriving in Agra. Someone said they had to run away from their homes and were chased by angry Indians. There's lots of whispering with serious faces among the grown-ups – you know the sort, frowns and furrowed brows – which stops as soon as a child or servant comes near. Who knows what they're talking about, and who cares?

I don't because I've got last night to roll around

my mind. Getting into trouble was a fair swap to see Romanini and Juliette. It's a balancing act isn't it – sometimes things are worth getting into trouble for. Maybe I should run away to the circus. Maybe Juliette will fall in love with a rich Nawab who will shower her with jewels to tempt her from the circus. Then I will take her place, swinging through the air with the Great Romanini.

My mouth creased upwards. I closed my eyes once more, willing my hither-and-thither mind to stay fixed on the most delicious daydream… me on a tightrope in a purple and gold costume, gesturing to Romanini, hair piled on top of my head. I have long bronze-red hair (and green eyes in case you're wondering – "Just like your mother, Grannie said").

"Bother, Bea."

I opened my eyes. He – Romanini – had gestured to me as we were leaving last night, Aunt Constance's bony hand wrapped tight around my wrist, tugging me along, the crowd parting to let us through, tutting and tsking as I passed. I looked back and the people melted away behind us to reveal him standing at the edge of the ring, one hand resting on the head of the tiger, Tonton, sitting beside him like a faithful dog with its master. Romanini raised his other hand and beckoned me.

"Come back," he mouthed. At least that's what I thought he said. What did he mean? Maybe he *did* mean *Run away and come join us in the circus*. I would be able to do it, I'm absolutely sure about that. I am far and away the best gymnast in school. I'm not being boastful, I'm being truthful and you're supposed to be truthful all the time aren't you? Even Aunt Constance can't disagree with me on that.

No one at school can do cartwheels like me, and what's more, back home I used to walk out along tree branches, with my arms stretched for balance, and hardly ever fell off.

Yes, it will take practice to get it right but I'll work hard, and concentrate equally hard. I can concentrate when I really, really want to, although I can't at school, not with everything they expect you to learn. Like sums or algebore. I do try. Sometimes. But when Miss Goodenough chalks on the board, say, $z + 2 - y = 17$, or whatever gobbledygook, there always seems something more interesting to think about. Like running off to join the circus.

"Hup," I said, leapt out of bed and walked on my

hands across to the window. A girl on our boat out to India said it looked like my legs were waving at her when I walked on my hands. I have long legs, which is probably a good thing. It is in Scotland, when it comes to wading across overflowing burns or peeking over walls.

I've never met anyone else who can walk on their hands. Can you? I suppose Romanini and Juliette would be able to. Perhaps having long fingers helps. I'm a long girl all over, Grannie says. Apart from my toes. I've got stumpy toes.

I taught myself to walk on my hands (so my feet and stumpy toes could have a rest). It was one long winter when we were snowed in, snow piled so deep along the glen nothing could move.

My, what I'd do for a fall of snow right now – how cooling it would be. At the window I sprang back to my feet with a flick of my body and arms and stared out the window.

The view was already boringly familiar. My room is at the back of the large bungalow and looks out on a dusty yard towards the back gate used by the servants. At the front, and out of sight, is a lawn and some straggly bushes. The lawn's divided by a path of crushed shells – to stop snakes slithering across – leading to the front gate where a soldier stands guard. Whether he's supposed to keep me in or others out I'm not at all sure.

I wish the Campbells lived properly in Agra, not out here in the British settlement, halfway to nowhere. As magistrate, Uncle Theophilus (I once called him Uncle Theo to the horror of Aunt C) could have had the pick of one of the grand old houses in the shadow of the great fort that towers over the city and so be right in the middle of it.

Agra seems to have a ceaseless hustle and bustle, its alleyways darting here and there before leading into great squares surrounded by cool marble palaces, and noise: lots and lots of voices, happy, sad, angry, laughing, yelling, the sound of life, everywhere around us but not including us. We remain separate.

Now I'm here, and here to stay whether I want to or not, I wish I could go and explore properly. I'm an explorer you see, that's why I'm wriggly, because I want to go and find new things. Instead all I get to see is on the walk to and from school, the same route every day, through the city gate and right just past the peculiar wall painting of a figure with an elephant's head and a chubby tummy, and always accompanied by the chowkidar, the night watchman. He escorts me and Primrose to school on his way home after his night's work. Then he's outside the school when the bell rings for leaving time, waiting to take us straight back to the bungalow, no detours, no stopping.

I've tried to ask him about the city. You can't close your eyes to what's going on around you. I mean how many shops at home have parakeets and canaries hanging in cages outside, screeching, tweeting and chirping as if trying to tempt customers in? Our morning route to school is a tease for the curious and I'm as curious as a prying cat. Bird-catchers push past, nets twitching with their early-morning haul; shopkeepers prepare for the day, opening shutters and yelling and shouting at each other as they lay out their goods; shoemakers and jewellers and moneylenders and grain merchants and butchers and bakers and, best of all, sweet-sellers. Peasants trudge in from the country with baskets filled with fruit that shines as if it's been polished. Children wearing next to nothing dart squealing around the streets, beggars shake their bowls and are shooed away by the well-to-do. On one corner there is a water-seller, on the next a tooth-cleaner with bundles of twigs and across from him a stern-looking man Primrose says is an ear-cleaner brandishing wicked-looking instruments.

I asked the chowkidar if that was true – did he really clean ears (sometimes I think Primrose is teasing me)? The chowkidar said nothing so I tried again. I asked him what was that building with its golden dome winking in the morning sun, who was that man with the snake wrapped around his neck (I really, truly saw that, walking past as if it was the height of normal)? There's another man we pass every morning leading two Persian cats who walk like princesses, seeing everyone as beneath them. So I asked about the cats and as always the chowkidar shook his head and said nothing.

It's against Uncle Theophilus's rules to talk to the servants unless you want something. All the British – and the rich Indians – have servants, and lots of them. That's the way it is in India. I have an old woman, she's called an ayah – she's really called Janaki because I asked and asked and at last she told me her name. Janaki brushes my hair, 100 strokes every morning, 100 strokes every evening.

She wouldn't talk to me at first in case Aunt

Constance overheard. So instead I talked at Janaki, just my babblings: Beatrice the Babbler, that's me when I get going, like a spring burn running over rocks. It's nice sometimes to have someone just listen to you. I told her about home and Grannie and how much I wanted to go back to her. One day I stopped and sniffed because I'd made myself sad and Janaki started singing, ever so quietly, so nobody outside my room would hear it.

She sang in her language so I didn't understand any of it but I knew what it meant. As she sang she went on brushing and I felt her voice cuddle me. I closed my eyes.

Afterwards I told her she had a beautiful voice and I wished she would sing and speak to me more. She sings to me in the evening now. A few nights ago I lay down and put my head on her lap and she smoothed my hair behind my ear as she sang.

I don't know anything about her because she won't say and I don't see her anywhere else but in my room. Where does she go? It's like she disappears in a puff of smoke.

Servants are always about but grown-ups look straight through them. I don't think they're considered people at all. Houses are built with extra staircases on the outside so the servants can get around without disturbing the memsahib, as the master of the house is called.

The governor, so Primrose told me, even has a servant to flick flies away from him and his wife when they are resting. Why would you do that? Primrose directed her most withering look at me in response.

"Really, Beatrice," she said. "Stop questioning everything."

I sighed. I keep asking her to call me Bea but she won't. I've started calling her Prim. It annoys her. Hurray!

Everything is 120 times different to home and I don't know what to make of it. On the boat coming out to India I had a pain in my stomach. They said it was because of sea sickness but I think it was anger with Mother and Father for dying and leaving me in this mess. I know it's still there inside me because sometimes I get this ache. I try not to think about it, or them if I can. I try really hard because sometimes bad things are best ignored for as long as possible.

"There's such a lot of everything," I wrote to Grannie. She encourages me to write letters to her, as long as

possible and telling her every detail of my new life. She says I'm good at writing things down because I see things in a different way to other people. I think Grannie just likes getting letters from me because she's lonely up there, getting old at the end of Glen Laddich all on her own.

"After church we go and walk in the grounds of this beautiful palace called the Taj Mahal. It's made of shiny white marble with tall towers and on top domes shaped like the smoothest, most perfect meringues you have ever seen and I don't think I've ever seen anything quite as beautiful. Miss Goodenough (she's my teacher, she's nice most of the time – I don't think teachers are allowed to be nice all the time) told me it was built by the old, old Emperor for his wife's tomb. She was called Mumtaz Mahal. They say it was a sign of his undying love for her but I said to Miss Goodenough wouldn't it have been a better sign of his undying love if he'd built a palace for her when she was alive so she would know of his undying love?

"There are orange trees in the palace garden – you can just reach up and pick an orange. Can you imagine that! But I'm not allowed to and I'm not allowed to climb the trees either. Uncle Theo (ha! I'm not allowed

to call him that!) says women must not eat oranges in public, only in our bedrooms because it is 'unbecoming'. What's unbecoming, Grannie?

"The other rules come from the governor (he's Very Important and is in charge of everyone and everything) and we must all follow them. The governor lives in the fort in Agra. It's like a fortress from a fairy tale with its huge battlements and turrets and towers. It glows when the sun sets on it. I call it the Red Castle. I've not been there yet but hope to go soon for a look around – I'm sure there will be lots to explore.

"I didn't want to like India, and still mean not to, because it took Mother and Father but I have to say it is a very colourful place, especially here in Agra. The ladies wear beautiful flowing robes of every colour in the whole world. They are called saris, they're like a cross between a light cloak, a kilt and a shawl. You should see their clothes and the men's splendid moustaches – I will do a drawing for you of an Indian man and an Indian woman so you can see just how splendid they are.

"Of course, booooooo, I am not allowed to dress like the Indian ladies. Their saris are light and thin and help to stop them getting too hot – I have to wear a dress every day and it's so, so hot. I'm a sweaty Betty all right.

On the way home from school every day we pass a pop shop that sells glasses of the most delicious-looking ginger beer. There are always soldiers there guzzling it down like there's no tomorrow. I'm sorry to say it looks even better than your lemonade. How I long to stop and drink, but no, of course not. It's against the Rules.

"So much colour Grannie, all around, but it's turned grey by the Rules. No one talks to me except to tell me what to do. Everyone speaks this strange language, English yes but with Indian words scattered through it and extra sprinkles of words that are made up, English words squashed together with Indian ones. Indish I suppose you could call it, or Englian.

"I have an ayah who is Janaki. She looks after me and I like her and I hope she likes me. I think she does. Prim and Proper (that's what I call Cousin Primrose) has one as well. At first Janaki called me Missie Baba, which is little girl, but I didn't like that so now she calls me Beatrice but says it her way. The children at school call me Griffin because that's what they call newcomers. I don't like that either – they say it in a nasty way. In mid-morning we have chota hazerie which is bread, butter and tea.

"When will I see Baby George, Grannie? Aunt

Constance just says 'in good time' when I ask her. I have to stay here to go to school because there are no schools in the station where George and Aunt Celia live many, many miles from here. Anyway, Aunt Constance says, Aunt Celia is very busy looking after Baby George, tho' I don't suppose he's a baby anymore. I don't think anyone really wants me here.

"Write to me, Grannie dearest. A letter from you would make me happy. This should be the adventure of my life – that's what you promised it would be – but it is the most boring part of my life ever. There might be wonderful things here I think but they always seem beyond my reach, always round the next corner and the rules, and Aunt C, forbid me from taking the smallest step towards discovering them.

"I know you say it's only the bore who gets bored so I will try and find an Adventure. I will – I promise.

"All my love and hugs, Bea xxx."

I let out a big sigh. Nothing stirred outside the window. Nothing stirred inside the house. It was midday, the hottest point of the day. It was like time stood still. I yawned.

I turned back to face the room and raised my arms. I was ringmaster at the circus.

"Welcome, ladies and gentlemen, boys and girls, to Aunt Constance's Circus, THE most boring place in the whole, ENTIRE WORLD."

3

I peered out the classroom window. The glass was dirty and dusty so there wasn't much to see. It had been a peculiar morning.

First of all when Janaki finished brushing my hair, she'd placed her hands on my shoulders. "May Vishnu protect you from all that is coming," she said and before I could ask who Vishnu was and what he might protect me from, she was gone, and she wasn't the only one.

The night watchman was nowhere to be found when it was time to walk to school. Aunt Constance tutted and went to look for the gardener: he could take us. She would not stand for her daughter and niece to be late. That wouldn't do at all.

The gardener was nowhere to be found. And

there was no guard on the gate. Aunt Constance went to fetch the carriage but the carriage boy was nowhere to be found. So Aunt Constance walked us to school herself with a good deal of tutting and muttering and a firm hold on our hands, all at a pace so brisk that I was breathless and even hotter than usual by the time we arrived. There was no sign of the man with his Persian cats today and the pop shop was shut.

I pulled at my dress where it stuck to my back. It was so hot. What I would have given for a ginger beer. Mind you at that moment even a glass of the dusty water they give us in school would have tasted as good as anything. I could imagine gulping it down then holding out the glass for another.

Sometimes I feel I'm a flower wilting in the heat; I just want to let my head drop because the effort of even holding it upright is too much. My head tipped forward, so hot, mustn't close my eyes. I wish I didn't have to go to school, I wish I was home, I wish I was cold. I wish I was…

KERRRRASSSSHHHH.

The front door to the school was heaved so violently open it made every single person within its walls jump. Miss Goodenough let out a gasp and, I'm ashamed to say, I squealed.

That was embarrassing but I'd been so far away, so lost in my own thoughts and not paying attention to Miss Goodenough's lesson that being brought back to earth with a crash gave me more of a fright than anyone else.

Everyone's eyes were fixed on the closed door to our classroom. One of the girls whimpered, Miss Goodenough flashed an encouraging smile but said nothing.

Heavy, booted footsteps galloped down the corridor then stopped outside the room. Now the classroom door flew open and in leapt two men in uniform, wearing the white jackets, tight white trousers and long black boots with jingling silver spurs of the cavalry.

"My sister – where's my sister?" barked the first of them, a short, squat, ruddy-faced young man with blond hair and a wispy blond moustache grown in an attempt to make him look older. Instead it looked as if he hadn't wiped his top lip properly after a drink of milk.

"Bertie! My goodness."

It was Martha Starling. She stood up and I saw she was an exact copy of her brother, only a few years younger and missing the milk moustache.

"Sit down please, Miss Starling," instructed Miss Goodenough, her voice as calming and commanding as always. She had that teacher's voice, the kind that meant you did what she said. A hubbub from the street pursued the two young officers and filled the classroom.

"Young men, this is a place of learning for young ladies. It is polite to knock before entering and polite to close a door behind you. Now kindly..."

"Martha – come on, there is no time... come..." Martha's brother strode down the class towards her, one hand outstretched, his face becoming redder with every stride. She took it and he yanked her after him.

The other officer drew his sword.

Have you ever heard a sword being drawn from a scabbard? It's a sound you will never forget; a sound you cannot forget. This was the first time I heard it. It's a clean, sharp scrape that makes the hairs on the back of your neck stand up. Because the drawing of a sword is a sign something dreadful is going to happen. The girls in the front row gasped.

"Starling," barked the other officer. "We must get them all out."

Starling said nothing but his answer was clear as he pushed past his fellow officer and hurried Martha out the door, down the corridor and away into the street.

"Well, I'll be damned," said the officer. I swallowed a giggle.

"Sir," said Miss Goodenough. "You will be good enough to mind your language in the company of ladies."

Before he could reply two more men came charging down the corridor and burst into the room. Us girls, well drilled by Miss Goodenough, remained seated at our desks.

"Excuse ME," said the teacher, her voice rising in a crescendo we knew spelt trouble for whoever was on the receiving end.

"*Sub lal hogea hai,*" roared one of the men. They were both wearing only baggy pairs of colourful trousers as if they'd been in too much of a hurry to finish dressing. It was not their trousers that demanded attention – it was the fact each was waving a jagged dagger around their heads.

"Well," snapped Miss Goodenough, who being as

keen to learn as she was to teach had taken lessons in Hindi. "Everything shall not run red in here... now get OUT."

To emphasise the point she hurled her wooden duster at the men just as the officer lunged at them with his sword.

"Harrrgghhh," said the officer and the men fled back into the street hooting with laughter.

"What on earth is going on?" wondered Miss Goodenough.

Whatever it was, I was thoroughly enjoying the show. This was much more like it – plenty to tell Grannie in my next letter home. It was too much for Euphemia Winter. There were three Winter sisters, all seated in the front row. Euphemia was the youngest. She groaned and tumbled to the ground.

I was the first to react. I leapt from my place in the third row and helped the swooning Euphemia back into her seat. I couldn't keep the grin off my face. The elder Winters gave me a frosty look.

"We must leave at once, Ma'am," said the remaining officer. "I must get you all to the fort – you'll be safe there."

"Thank you, Beatrice. Safe from what?"

"Rebellion, Ma'am, the Indian soldiers, they're up in arms, say they're going to kill all the foreigners – *maro feringhi, maro feringhi,* they're all yelling it. We'll be safe in the fort until it all dies down and everyone comes to their senses."

"And when will that be? The girls have a spelling test this afternoon."

"Begging your pardon, Ma'am, this is no time for a spelling test..."

"Hurray!" It was out of my mouth before I could stop myself, and much louder than I meant it to be.

"That's a final warning, Miss Spelling," said Miss Goodenough. She clapped her hands together. "Come girls, in pairs, follow me – the officer will bring up the rear."

"I should go first, Ma'am – I have a sword."

"And I, sir, have a rolled umbrella – that will be more than enough."

I took Euphemia's hand and hurried out to the front. I wanted to be in the first pair so I would have first look at whatever was going on outside.

To start with, not much. The narrow street outside the school had resumed its usual stillness, and was as baking hot as ever.

Holding tight to Euphemia's sweaty hand, I marched after Miss Goodenough as we crossed a quiet square and headed up a lane leading towards the main road that sweeps in through the great gates and heads up to the fort. There was a rumbling from its direction that grew louder as we approached. A cloud of dust covered the corner where our lane met the main street. I stepped past Miss Goodenough and into the street to get a better look, tugging Euphemia along.

Euphemia whimpered once more and then yelped as I hauled her back.

"Girls!" warned Miss Goodenough.

Just in time. A camel shambled past, then another and another. They had furniture piled on their backs and their enormous loads looked like they could come crashing down at any second.

The other girls pressed against me and Euphemia, trying to see what was going on. Euphemia pressed back against the girls, wanting them to surround her. I stared, open-mouthed like a toddler. This, I told myself, had the makings of a very fine adventure indeed.

Behind the camels came two heavily-laden carts pulled by huge bullocks plodding up in the direction of the fort.

And around the carts and the camels were people, lots and lots of people, splashes of red among them marking the presence of soldiers, and from all the men, women, children, animals, large and small, rose a relentless hullabaloo. Shouting, screaming, bellowing, snorting, the clank-clunk of wooden wheels on the cobbles, all stirred together and brought to the boil by the heat of the day.

From the far side of the road there was the sound of something being smashed and more screams, louder, more urgent, screams of alarm. I took another step back. My classmates had already done the same. The noise filled my ears, dust rose from the road and filled my mouth, tried to get down my throat. I coughed. It was difficult to breathe, difficult to... a face darted in front of mine, a boy, about my age, his dark hair sticking out all over the place.

"Haaahhh," he said and I jumped. "You English, you're finished – when our army arrive from Delhi they'll cut you and all the others into tiny pieces."

The boy chopped his hands up and down to demonstrate the fate he predicted for me, Euphemia, Miss Goodenough, the other girls, and, no doubt, for George, Aunt Celia and her husband and all the others who'd left home to chase fame and fortune in India.

"The sepoys are rebelling," said the boy. "They won't take your orders no more. Your soldiers aren't your soldiers and the weapons you gave them will be aimed at you! No more telling people what to do."

"I never did," I snapped back, leaning away as the boy danced in front of me so close that if I'd stuck out my tongue I could have licked his nose. He was hopping from one foot to the other, pulling faces and all the time making chopping sounds as he waved his hands in accompaniment to his threats.

"Shooo! Be off with you," ordered Miss Goodenough and pushed at the boy.

He took a step back and pointed at Miss Goodenough. “And you,” he said, “chop, chop, chop.”

A surge of people hurrying up the street swept the boy away. He came from nowhere and in seconds he was back there.

I glanced at Euphemia and could tell she was trying not to cry. How could I tell? Because I was the same. The boy’s performance had shoved my sense of adventure out on to the road where I watched it being squashed flat by the yellow-toothed camels and a mass of panicking people. What was going on? The butterflies that fluttered in my tummy when I thought something exciting was going to happen had vanished. Instead an altogether different feeling was trying to take over my stomach, legs, arms, and most of all my head. FEAR. I was frightened, frightened like I’d never been frightened before.

4

It took over an hour of struggling through the crowded streets – at one point Miss Goodenough used her umbrella and prodded and poked a clear path – for us to reach the safety of the fort. I held tight to Euphemia's hand all the way and she held tight to mine. My mouth was dry, my heart racing. The heat, the noise, people everywhere, pressed tight together; it felt difficult to breathe.

As we hurried across the fort's drawbridge and through the colossal gates, guarded by a clutch of shaky soldiers, cannons scowling through the loopholes on either side, I glanced back and caught the officer's sword glinting in the sunlight as he waved the final pair of girls through. Or what he thought was the final pair.

"Shut the gates, shut the gates," he barked at the soldiers.

I let go of Euphemia's hand and looked around.

"Prim?"

I searched the gaggle of girls gathered just inside the gates.

"Primrose?"

I turned and ran, pushed past the officer and darted back out into the crowded square.

"No... wait... come back..."

The officer's commands chased me across the drawbridge. He didn't. He remained where he was, waving his sword in a threatening manner at no one in particular. Someone in the crowd laughed at him.

By now I was in the crowd. They didn't pay much attention to me, being too busy enjoying the sight of the British, flush-faced and full of panic, fleeing to the fort in case the rebelling Indian soldiers should arrive from Delhi. A couple of children skipped along beside me yelling "Make way for the *feringhi*, make way *feringhi baba* coming through," and then laughing at the fun of it all.

I didn't find it much fun. My head was pounding, so much noise, so hot, so much dust, my eyes blinking madly and making tears stream down my cheeks. Face after face turned to look at me as I pushed past, some jumped in my way then out of it, just as I felt panic seizing me. A hand fell on my shoulder; I yelped, prompting a peel of laughter around me.

Where was Primrose? I had to find her. I could see the top of the fountain that marked the midpoint of the square and made for it.

There they were, Primrose and one of the other Winter sisters, backed against the base of the fountain. They seemed frozen, too terrified to move an inch. People around them were staring and pointing.

Primrose was making a strange sound, mewing like a frightened kitten. An old woman put a hand out to try to comfort her. Primrose shied away from her.

"Come on." I pushed my way between the girls. They looked at me wide-eyed and somehow that made me feel better. I had to take control; it was down to me to get us to the fort.

"Come on," I said again and hooked an arm behind

each girl's elbow. Head down, I forced my way back through the crowd. Faces peered in at us, a blur of eyes and mouths; mouths moving and yelling, hooting and mocking. But not a single person touched us.

"Get out the way!" I shouted with everything I had left and pushed onwards. The old woman was close behind us. She was scaring me. Primrose was still mewing.

"Thammo!" The old woman started shouting… but it wasn't at us. *"Hut jao! Hut jao!"*

The crowd fell quiet and parted; a path opened to the fort. The Winter sister stumbled but I gripped hard and stopped her from falling – if we stopped or fell, I was terrified the crowd would close around us and we'd never make the fort.

The officer was still on the drawbridge, waving his sword in an unconvincing attempt to discourage the crowd from coming any closer, his face drained of colour.

"Quick," he barked.

"Well, I'm not exactly trying to go slowly," I snapped as we rushed past him. We scuttled through the gates. They closed behind us and nothing was ever the same again.

❖

I didn't know that then. Of course not. It's possible to predict the future when each day is the same as the one before, school, home, school, home, boredom, boredom, boredom. But at a time like that nobody could know what's around the next corner.

Thankfully after that dreadful first day, the fear, a peculiar feeling that tingles and threatens to take away any ability to think or move – it's true you really can be frozen with fear, I think Primrose nearly was – slithered away with each day that passed.

Because that's what can happen, whether you're a bored schoolgirl or a gnarled old soldier: the odd or the different or even the scary becomes the everyday if it happens every day.

We were under siege, trapped in the fort by Indian soldiers who had risen in rebellion with more on the way, a whole army some said. I expected a siege to be like something out of Miss Goodenough's history book – *The Kings and Queens of England* – when knights in shining armour had hot oil poured on them from the battlements and vast siege machines hurled chunks of stone against castle walls.

But no one threw or shot anything at the fort. I did see one battle. It happened outside the fort and that really did seem like we were watching a history book brought to life.

I sneaked on to the battlements where the soldiers' worried wives were and watched the distant puff of guns and the flashes of colour as the red-coated soldiers charged this way and that.

Later we watched our defeated soldiers retreat to the fort, saw the wounded carried in, groaning and bloodied. I saw Martha Starling's brother on one stretcher; his eyes were shut and he didn't look very alive. Is losing a brother worse than losing a mother or father? I looked around for Martha but could see no sign of her.

I was glad my brother was still a bairn and too young to fight. There was no news about him.

There was very little news about anything. In its place people needed to have something to talk about and in a siege, when you're cut off, gossip and rumour are the only things there's no shortage of. It's like the playground at school. You have to work out who you believe and what to believe.

On the one hand, no news might be good news

because lists of the dead had reached the fort and there was no George Spelling among the names. On the other hand, no news could be bad news because there was a widely held view among the grown-ups that anybody not in the fort was at the mercy of the rebels and so as good as dead. There was whispered talk of massacres.

For once I followed the advice of Aunt Constance and ignored all rumours. Soon enough there were other things to occupy me, including some bad news that turned out to be all too true. Miss Goodenough set up a makeshift classroom and a few weeks later than planned delivered the postponed spelling test (I hadn't revised and came second bottom of the class ahead of only Euphemia Winter, who hadn't been the same since the day we fled to the fort). The eldest Winter sister started calling me "Beatrice Spulling" which everyone thought was ever so funny. Then they started calling me "Silly Spulling". I couldn't seem to do anything right in their eyes.

At least the school day was shorter – just the morning in class – after which I could escape Primrose, the Winters and all the other girls and go off to explore on my own. The red fort was vast, like a walled city with palaces, dark alleys, bright squares, gardens where cattle and sheep were left to graze, and corridors and tunnels that went here, there and who knows where.

At its highest point the fort was crowned by a tower that offered a view over Agra and across the grey, sluggish Jumna, the vast river that came to life hundreds of miles to the north and merged with two more to become the mighty Ganges hundreds more to the south.

It was from the tower that I watched the city burn. After winning the battle the rebels surged into the streets and began to help themselves to anything they could find in the abandoned houses. When they were done they set fire to the houses. The night sky was lit by flames.

I spent the night curled up in a blanket on the battlements, scared by the thought of being caught in a burning building. The next morning discarded furniture from the looted homes floated down the Jumna. Up above, the great fort scowled down on it all, its walls too tall and too thick for the rebels' guns. We couldn't get out, they couldn't get in.

That night I returned to the room I shared with

Aunt Constance, Uncle Theophilus, Primrose, the three Winter sisters and their mother. Me and Primrose slept head to toe in a thin army cot – each time she moved it woke me – with its legs in bowls of water because Primrose was scared of ants or cockroaches getting into our bed. The windowless room was cramped and smelly, although at least the double door opened on to the Diwan-i-Khas garden which made it a slightly better place to live than Miss Goodenough's gloomy room in the Gunsheds.

Next door to us were the Murrays. Wee Archie Murray screamed in his sleep because, so his big sister told me, the Murrays had seen one of the massacres when the rebellion began and had only escaped with their lives thanks to their ayah and cook smuggling them to safety.

On the other side was Mr Blake the missionary and a brother and sister, Master and Miss Misst, whose parents had disappeared without trace.

There were all sorts packed into the fort, from many different countries and places, like a Noah's Ark for humans. There were plenty of Indian people who sided with the British but the governor did nothing to reward their choice. They had to make their own shelters on top of the existing buildings, from where they watched the bustle down below and, as their empty stomachs rumbled, wondered if they'd picked the wrong side.

In Block C there were 20 singing nuns from France. I liked to listen to them practising, conducted by their ferocious Mother Superior. Madame St Bruno she was called. But you had to be careful because if the Mother Superior found a child where she thought they shouldn't be (which was anywhere but the schoolroom) she would grab the nearest ear, twist it and march the offender back on tiptoes. My ear hurt for two days after she caught me looking for eggs in the corner of the garden where the chickens pecked and scratched their days away.

Which is pretty much what everyone was doing while we waited for the British army to arrive from Lucknow and save us. Days passed, weeks went by, a month meandered past. The food was rationed – we had to queue for our share each morning. What we were given wasn't much to look at and didn't taste of much either. Then we washed up because for once there were no servants and washed our clothes and sometimes even ourselves – we had to be careful with water so once a week we were allowed a quick dip in a barrel filled to halfway. We had to share the water between a couple of families and, let me tell you, you did not want to be the last person in.

All this time the baking heat of the Indian day beat down, raising the temperature, shortening tempers and draining the will to do anything but stare at the marbled walls. Sometimes I would sit and stare and stare at a lizard on the wall. Where did they come from? No matter how long you watched they never moved. They were just there. Then they weren't.

The biggest battle, it turned out, was not resisting invaders, it was with boredom. AGAIN. My, do I hate being bored!

For a time, I went and watched the soldiers on their daily march up, down and around the parade ground. Sometimes I took water to them as they stood guard on the ramparts, staring out across the hot, dusty plain far below and all the time wishing they were anywhere else but India. Me too.

Private Coombe, a chatty young man from London, decided he would teach me to charge and load a musket and pistol. "All ladies in here should," he said with an emphatic nod. "Just in case."

"Just in case what?" I wondered.

"In case," said Coombe and began his lesson.

One day Uncle Theo – it felt too much effort to give him his full name – took Aunt Con, me and Prim to be introduced to the Gov. He was serving tea for his staff and their families in his rooms (two big rooms all to himself I noted).

Theophilus Campbell was one of the governor's most trusted advisers. I watched him as he bent over the governor's desk studying a report. He stood up.

"First case?"

"Indeed," said the governor.

"There will be more, if this disease spreads..."

"Indeed," said the governor and added a cough as a full stop as he noticed my interest.

"Young lady," he said. "Eavesdropping is not what an English lady does."

I opened my mouth and shut it again when I caught Uncle Theo's thunderous stare. So I gave the governor my very best curtsey (that should quieten the old buffer) and swung my gaze away from the men. A servant boy was standing behind the governor's chair. He was about my age if a little taller. He stood parade-ground straight, a crisp white turban on his head to match the baggy white shirt and trousers he wore.

I wondered lazily what his job could be and as I watched him I realised the blank expression worn by so many servants (never let the memsahib know what you're thinking) had vanished. Instead he was grinning at me beneath dark, twinkling eyes. He stood stock still, as he was supposed to, but you could sense the energy within him, his twitchiness – he looked desperate to burst into life.

I began to offer a grin back only to be interrupted by the boy sticking his tongue out at me. Did he? My mouth dropped open in surprise. This was not how servants were supposed to behave.

"Goodness, Beatrice, close your mouth – you look like a simpleton," said Aunt Constance.

The boy, enjoying my telling-off, winked at me and stuck his tongue out again. I scowled back, prompting Aunt Constance to swivel round to seek the target of my attention. In an instant the servant boy's face was deadpan and Aunt Constance never even noticed him.

5

It was a Sunday, about mid-afternoon on a day sweltering even by Agra's standards, that I discovered the hidden courtyard.

In the time we'd been shut up in the fort I'd given myself a mission to explore as much as I could. I would map the fort; from the great halls and once lavish pavilions, where in centuries gone by the old Emperor and his many wives and children had lived their sheltered existence, to the soldiers' barracks and rooms filled with nothing but cannon balls.

My favourite expedition was to disappear into one of the covered alleyways and then duck into one of the tunnels or passages that led off and see where I ended up. I'd emerge into tykhanas, gloomy underground rooms that looked like nobody had set foot in them for centuries. Tykhanas were built for the hottest time of the year as they were much cooler than the rooms above ground. Every night on returning from my expeditions I drew each newly discovered room and tunnel on my map.

Some days I got into trouble and was chased away by angry soldiers because I was somewhere I shouldn't be. On another I found myself in the fort's hospital, rows of thin beds filled by groaning men and the whole place coated with a horrible, sickly smell. I held my breath and looked for Martha Starling's brother but couldn't see him anywhere. One soldier, a bandage wrapped around his head and more on his hands and arms, called out as I passed.

I bent close to him as his voice was faint and scratching. "Sing for us, lassie," he said, so I sang, as brightly as I could, one of the songs Grannie taught me about bluebells smelling sweet where my highland laddie dwells, until an orderly appeared and shooed me away.

There were all sorts of different tunnels, a warren of the well-trod and long forgotten. Some of the ones I explored were pretty grand to be called tunnels. They were somewhere between corridors, walkways and alleyways. You could stand upright and they had cobbled floors but everyone called them tunnels. So tunnels they were.

The deeper they went the smaller they became, more like you'd imagine a proper tunnel to be. Some were rumoured to lead out of the fort and were said to be used by the governor's spies to smuggle in vital information. When I suggested that must also mean rebel spies could get in, I was told not to be such a "silly girl".

I kept to the bigger tunnels (unless I took a wrong turning). Truth be told I was a little scared of the dark and there was no way I was ready to scuttle off down some deep, dark, narrow tunnel – I might bump into a merciless mutineer spy and who knows what else. Snakes, rats for sure. A ghost?

I shuddered at the thought and followed my chosen passage of the day. Ahead, a bright light signalled its end.

The passage opened into a covered walkway surrounding a square, dusty courtyard. It had an air of long-gone glory. The carvings on the walkway's pillars were chipped and uncared for. There was an elephant that had lost its trunk, and part of one tusk. Actually on closer examination I realised it wasn't an elephant at all. It was like the wall painting down in the city, the one that meant we should turn right for school. It had the head of an elephant but it was on top of a man's body – a man with a large tummy. He seemed to have four arms as well, one of which stretched towards me as if it was offering me something. I shook my head; the heat could make you think squint. I looked around. A rope was tied tight across the courtyard. It ran diagonally, secured between two of the corner pillars.

I stepped into the courtyard and blinked at the brightness. I pulled at the rope. It gave a little but felt secure.

"I wonder," I said out loud. I like talking to myself. Always have. Makes you feel you have a friend with you.

I climbed on to the top of the railing that separated the walkway from the courtyard and held on to the pillar. I put one foot on the rope and tested it.

"No different to tree walking in Glen Laddich," I said with a confidence I didn't feel. I swung the other foot on to the rope as well. Still I clung on to the pillar.

"One, two, three..."

I let go and slowly stretched my arms out.

"Yes," I said, feeling myself find my balance. "Off we go... the amazing, double-daring Acrobat from Ardnamurchan."

I lifted my back foot and swung it round in front of me, lifted the other foot and placed that back in front, then another step. Deep breath. Keep my breathing regular. Slow and deep. I was doing it. My arms circled, trying to keep my balance. I swayed, but only a little. This was fine. Then I swayed a little more and stopped. Oh no I was going to...

"You should not stop – especially when you are a beginner."

I looked up sharply. The voice came from the far side, from the darkness of the walkway.

"I'm no beginner," I snapped and fell off.

I managed to put my hands out as I toppled, and as the rope was no more than hip-high it was not a significant fall. It was high enough to hurt, though. My hands and wrists took the brunt of it and a mouthful of dust added to the pain. My eyes pricked with tears. Embarrassing.

I spat out the dust, keeping a firm hold on my tears. I would not cry.

"Here, let me help you…"

I could feel the roughness of the dirt covering half my face. I looked up.

A hand reached towards me. I ignored it and pushed myself on to my knees.

"You?" I said, unable to keep the surprise from my voice.

"Who are you?" said the boy, flicking a lock of dark hair from his face.

"Bea, Beatrice Spelling… I saw you, saw you fly, just before…"

"Before what?"

"Before all this." I waved my hand around. "You know, war, the siege, this…"

I waved my hand again just to be sure he understood.

"The death-defying Romanini and Julietterrrr." Pronouncing it just as the ringmaster had. I couldn't stop myself.

I looked around the walkway. "Julietterrrr… where is she?"

The Great Romanini shrugged and walked away.

"Wait," I said, leaping to my feet and following. "Wait for me, Great Romanini..."

I giggled at the rhyme and skipped after him. "Romanini," I said again. "I can't believe it's you."

"Don't call me that." He stepped out of the sunlight into the shade of the walkway and dropped down on a heap of cushions piled in the north-west corner. Beneath the cushions a carpet covered part of the walkway. Decorated with swirls and twirls, it looked ready to fly away at any moment should a fairy-story princess need carrying to a happy ending.

There was a table and chair, handsomely carved, and a charpoy, a small Indian bed, on which a blanket was folded neatly. At its foot was a chest, which was ornate enough that it could have once belonged to an Indian prince. A jewel winked in the middle of its lid. There was no sign of Juliette.

"What is this place?"

He ignored my question, closing his eyes.

I spat on the ground. I couldn't get the dust out of my mouth.

"Urrrgghh," I said. "Sorry."

I wiped my mouth.

"Where is Juliette? I'd very much like to meet her."

I looked quizzically at Romanini. This time he looked back, narrowed eyes staring from beneath his dark fringe of hair, a look that said he did not want me here and he did not want anything to do with the rest of the world. I was *not* wanted.

He shouldn't have needed to add words. But this was me he was dealing with, and, in the words of Grannie, "Miss Beatrice Spelling has a well-maintained habit of doing what others don't want her to do."

"Go away."

He was forced to try words where his look had failed. They didn't work either.

"How long have you been here? Are you all in here, you know the circus, the magicians, the jugglers, the clowns… Ha! That would cheer everyone up, seeing the clowns wandering around looking sad at being under siege."

I giggled at the thought – imagine clowns fighting a battle! – and sat down next to Romanini on the cushions.

"In fact, what about doing a circus show – that would be fandabulous…"

Sometimes when I get excited my words struggle

to keep up with my thoughts. They don't always come out quite right, as if some of them take a wrong turning on the way from my brain to my mouth and end up in my ears.

"You've already the rope here… you and Juliette could do your act in the courtyard… no, wait, how many people could get in here, we'd need a bigger space… where is Juliette? Actually, maybe, maybe… would you two teach me? I'm good, better than just now. Would you? Would you teach me, Romanini… oh please say yes? Yes?"

I turned towards him, struggling to sit up amongst the softness of the cushions. He looked away and mumbled something.

"What?"

"I said I won't teach you anything and neither will Vette."

"Vette? Who is Vette? Oh, Juliette, that's your name for her, or Juliette is her Big Top name. I'm right aren't I? Oh please, Romanini… or is that your Big Top name as well? I'll ask Vette – she looks so nice I'm sure she'll say yes."

Romanini sprang to his feet with a flick of his legs and set off round the walkway.

"Wait." I scrambled out of the cushions. "Look… I could do it."

I flipped myself into the courtyard and walked across it on my hands.

"See?" I said. "Look – look at me…"

Romanini walked on.

"Oh for goodness sake." I was still walking on my hands. I raised my voice. "WHAT IS THE MATTER WITH YOU, ROMANINI, YOU GREAT FLYING GRUMP?"

My shout echoed around the courtyard, I lost my balance and for the second time in a few minutes sprawled in the dust. The strange trunkless elephant looked down on me – he could have at least used one of his four hands to help me up. Romanini stopped. He was next to the pillar around which one end of his tightrope was fixed. He rested his head against the pillar. I stood up and took a step towards him.

"Where is she… where is Vette?" My voice was low. Inside my head I scolded myself. "Oh, Bea, you've done one of your blunders again, haven't you, you silly little girl. You're such a child."

"Dead."

He spoke so quietly I wasn't sure what he said. I

knew what I thought he'd said. Only I didn't want to believe it. I wanted a different answer so I tried again.

"Where is Vette, Romanini?"

He looked up at me, eyes on mine. They blazed for a moment then went dark again.

"Dead." This time his word was firm, and final.

"Oh."

Dead. Firm and final. Gone forever. Like Mother and Father. That angry rumble stirred in my stomach. I swallowed hard. "But Julietterrr could fly."

I don't think the Great Romanini heard me.

"Disease… cholera, they said… one day she was well and making me practise our act. 'Soon we will be away from this fort and the show will go on, so come Jacques, allezzz hupppp'."

His voice lifted for the "allezzz hupppp" and he said it again, this time his voice falling and falling so it sounded as if he never finished.

"Your name is Jacques?"

Jacques nodded. "That morning she said she was not feeling well. By the evening she'd a fever, a bad fever. 'Help me, Jacques,' she said. She was burning. They were her last words to me. I ran, ran to that hospital for the soldiers and I begged and pleaded for a doctor to come with me and they wouldn't come. They wouldn't come… nobody would come. 'Fly away little Frenchie,' they said. When I got back, she… she was… she asked me, her big brother, asked me for help and I couldn't help her… I couldn't help her…"

He sniffed.

I looked around. "Here?"

Jacques shook his head and sniffed again. "I came here after – we had a room…" he waved his hand "… somewhere in the fort. We found this place and she got hold of the rope – it's the one we use in our act. When it started, this war, we were heading for Delhi, our next show. Vette and me, we'd been late leaving – Vette was always late. The others went on. Kamal the fire-eater said we could catch them up. He was cross with us. Not seen him or any of them since. When we got on to the road a soldier told us to ride for the fort – we were one of the last carriages to get in. Us and Tonton, all that's left of the circus I think. And the Top – that's still standing.

"Vette said we 'ad to go on, we owed it to the others to keep the show going so we 'ad to keep practising and come up with new, more daring, more 'death-defying' things for our act. It doesn't matter now because she couldn't defy death. Death has won."

His voice sounded very French, and very sad.

"No," I said. "No, it has not. You're still alive and Vette would want you to go on – that's what you said isn't it? The show must go on."

Jacques shook his head. "So now you know Vette do you? You know my sister?"

"Oh," I said, raising my hand to cover my mouth. I wanted to push my words back where they came from. "I didn't mean… I mean I didn't…"

"I want you to go," said Jacques. He turned and walked back to his corner.

"Jacques… sorry."

My apology fell short of the retreating French boy. "GO," he said, throwing the dismissal over his shoulder.

6

The thing Jacques didn't know about me – not yet – was that I don't take "go" for an answer. I did at first, retracing my steps through the passage, pausing to find a broken piece of stone and using it to make a small "x" besides the passage entrance. That night I lay in bed staring into the darkness and thinking, Primrose's toes by my ear, twitching in time with her dainty snores.

About a year or so ago I'd had one of my fireside chats with Grannie. They happened every now and then, when I couldn't sleep and came shivering down the chilly stairs to find her sitting by the crackling fire – its noise alone was enough to make you feel warmer. We huddled together, staring into the soothing flames, drinking hot milk as a storm drummed its presence on the window. Grannie was quiet and I asked her what the matter was. She sighed and began speaking about sadness; she'd lost a husband as well as a daughter: my grandfather. He died long before I was born.

I didn't listen to all of what she said – sorry Grannie but you know me. I do remember her saying there's nothing wrong with being sad. Some days you are, and sometimes it's for an obvious reason. Like remembering your mother and father are no longer around. Or your sister is gone. On other days, sadness folds itself around you for no reason in particular and that's fine too. Just so long as you don't let it become you.

Grannie was right, I thought, and so was Vette. She understood that; things happen, good or bad, and life goes on. Life always goes on for the living. It must. Otherwise what would be the point? Yes, I decided, I would go back and see Jacques, tomorrow or the next day. He couldn't be left alone.

"Yes," I said in a firm whisper. "The Great Romanini's show will go on."

"Shhh," hissed Aunt Constance.

I stuck my tongue out in the darkness. The servant boy sprung into my mind and I smiled at the memory.

What a funny thing to do. The smile faded and I sighed. I was lonely. There – I'd admitted it.

It's a feeling that had crept up on me ever since I left home. Like Grandmother's Footsteps. Every time I looked round there it was, a little closer. There had been a couple of children, Lottie and James, on the long voyage out to India – more than a month at sea on a stuffy, smelly boat – who I thought could be friends. When the boat arrived in Calcutta they stayed in the city with their mother and father. Lottie asked if I could stay with them because I was an orphan and needed a mother and father. "No dear," said her mother. "That's not the done thing." So instead I was sent up the long road to Agra, in the care of a Miss Sithart, a pale, frightened lady who was on the way to Meerut to get married.

On the hot, sweaty, uncomfortable journey in our horse-drawn gharry watching this strange, shimmering land pass slowly by, I tried and tried to convince myself I was going on an *adventure* like Grannie promised I would be. It would make the most amazing story to write for her. And all the time I tried and tried not to think it would be rather better to have an adventure with someone by my side.

As my teeth rattled on that rutted road to Agra, I pinned my hopes on my cousin. Yes, I actually pinned my hopes on Primrose. She would become like a sister, I thought, like the ones I read about in Grannie's books. We'd be side-by-side through thick and thin. I know that sounds silly now. And then just to top it all, the other girls in school were as icy about me as Prim and Proper and showed no signs of thawing.

"We don't like Griffins, and we certainly don't like chatterbox Scotch Griffins with carrot heads," announced the oldest Winter sister after the first school morning in the fort, when I suggested we go exploring our strange new home together.

Like being sad, there's nothing wrong with being on your own some of the time. I like being on my own a lot of the time. I'm used to it. But I want… No, I'll tell you what I *don't* want first. I don't want to be talking to myself forever. I want someone to hear me. I want… I want a friend.

I sighed again. Another thought popped into my head. I often find getting to sleep difficult because lying in bed is when so many thoughts, good, bad, interesting and silly, introduce themselves.

I turned on my side and screwed my eyes shut. I'd

settled on a final thought for the day: I was going to think about becoming an acrobat with Jacques – he wasn't that much older than me and was certainly just as alone. He would teach me in the hidden courtyard and I would practise, practise, practise until I could walk from one end of the tightrope to the other. And that would only be the beginning…

"No, non, non, non."

Jacques was not pleased to see me when I turned up two days later (I'd forced myself to wait a whole two days to allow him time to be sad – which was extra difficult because I'd wanted to go back as soon as I woke the morning after my first visit).

I scampered along the passage to the secret courtyard – without the "x" I would have taken an age to find it – well done me – and was surprised to find nobody at home. I sank down on the cushions to wait and when I grew bored of waiting I decided to give the tightrope a try.

"Wish me luck," I said to the elephant head.

Chewing my lip in concentration I let go of the pillar and stepped out. My eyes narrowed against the sunlight as I fixed my gaze on the far pillar. "Don't look down," I said and looked down.

Owww.

I picked myself up, dusted myself down and started again.

"Don't look down."

I arched my shoulders, kept myself as tall as I could, which was pretty tall for a girl my age, and off I went.

And I was going well, was going to make it all the way across (I really was), until Jacques returned and knocked me off with his negative thoughts.

"Non, non, non, non…"

"Aaarrrggghhhh."

Thump.

"Ow."

"Non, non, non…"

"All right I get the picture."

I studied the cut on my knee, blew on it, caught myself after one "tut" – I didn't want to turn into Aunt Constance – and stood up. I lifted my chin and marched out of the courtyard as if I was Private Coombe on parade. Left, right, left, right.

"There's an orange on the table for you."

I threw the words back at Jacques. A happy Private

Coombe had gifted it to me that morning – he'd been sent on patrol to the Taj Mahal and harvested a helmet-full. I think he'd adopted me because I had no father.

After school the next day I returned to the secret courtyard. Jacques was lying on his charpoy, legs tucked up, facing the wall.

"Bonjour Jacques," I said in my best bright-and-breezy voice. "I've come to practise."

Without pausing to let him answer I kicked off my shoes, took up position on the tightrope and tried again. I managed most of the way across before mounting excitement at the thought I was going to do it caused me to miss my step – see, I can admit when I make a mistake. Down I went, this time catching the rope as I fell which at least allowed me to land on my feet. It still hurt.

I tried again. "If at first you don't succeed…" The story of Robert the Bruce, the fugitive King of Scots and the persistent spider was one of Grannie's favourites. I knew it backwards. "Try, try, try again…"

I stepped out on to the tightrope. So did that make me the Bruce or the spider? I swung my back leg in front of me and felt the rope dig into my foot. It hurt

– my feet were soft. It would be easier to do this if I was a spider. And harder if I was the Bruce. Because he would be in armour. Now that would be a trick worth seeing – someone tightrope-walking in armour.

Concentrate, Bea, concentrate. Too late.

I missed the rope as I fell and twisted my ankle with a pained yelp.

I stared at the faded blue sky. The sun had disappeared behind the tall walls of the secret courtyard. Not a single window looked down on us. Just the elephant head. I could have sworn he was grinning at me. My ankle throbbed. My mouth was dry.

"You should go barefoot about the fort – it'll harden your feet."

I said nothing but as I clambered on to the rope once more, holding tight to the pillar, I snatched a guarded glance in the direction of Jacques' corner. He was sitting cross-legged on the charpoy watching me from beneath his dark fringe. It was as if he used his hair to hide behind.

Off I went again, arms outstretched, shoulders back. "Posture, Beatrice Spelling, posture," Miss Goodenough used to say when she spotted me slouching in class. When you're tall and bendy it's difficult not to slouch.

Miss Goodenough would make me walk up and down the rows of desks balancing a book on my head while the lesson went on around me. The rest of the girls never seemed to slouch – they'd probably got iron bars sewn into their corsets. Which was just the sort of silly thing people here would do; probably one of the governor's rules.

I was over halfway across. Step, swing of the leg, step, swing of the leg… Uh-oh, my arms began to flap. I knew what was coming so jumped off.

"I have to feed Tonton." Jacques was heading for the passage. I noticed he was barefooted.

"I'll come?" I said, adding a question mark with a tilt of my voice.

"Non," said Jacques. He stopped at the entrance to the passage and turned round. "You stay… and practise."

Jacques was a strict teacher. When I fell off, which I still did to add to my growing collection of bruises, he clapped his hands and shouted "Alllezzz huuuppp."

In reply I muttered the rudest word I could think of – the soldiers liked to teach me new ones – and then pulled myself back on to the rope.

"It is best to start before you are ten years of age, but that cannot be 'elped." Sometimes Jacques lost his English h's to his French accent. "So you 'ave much work to do. You must 'ave a strong back and rigid legs."

I could now walk from one end of the tightrope to the other, swivel and walk back again without falling off (mostly).

"So," instructed Jacques. "Keep your eyes fixed on a

spot – pick something before you begin walking and keep your eyes always on it. Do not even dare to blink – it is like you're 'ipnotised..."

"Like what?"

"'Ipnotised."

"My hips are tied?"

"Non, non – 'ipnotised, like tic-toc, tic-toc, you are under my spell..."

"Ah, hypnotised."

"Oui, that is what I said. Now pay attention – it is like you are 'ipnotised, nothing else in your head. You are alone – just you, never mind all those eyes fixed on you from the crowd, it is just you, you and the tightrope. You must feel it through your feet. When you are on the wire, up high, looking down on the world, you can never make a mistake – never – not one."

My mistakes got fewer and fewer and my feet became harder and harder. Each morning I set off for school with Primrose and three mornings a week I never made it to school. I had Primrose tell Miss Goodenough I was sick – lots of people were getting sick in the fort. That's what happens when you're under siege with dwindling supplies of food, medicine and people not being able to keep themselves clean. We were all pretty smelly.

It took all my persuasive powers to make Primrose cover for me. Of course Prim and Proper didn't want to but I reminded my dear cousin how I'd rescued her and saved her life (which was a wee bit sort of true). I also promised Primrose every orange Private Coombe brought back from his patrols and to do her washing for two weeks. It was the last offer that swung her.

I hid my shoes and skipped off to the hidden courtyard to meet Jacques, my other teacher. We practised all day – I wore a bonnet, one of Prim's, to keep the worst of the sun off my head and tied it around my chin to stop it coming off when I did somersaults.

Now I'd mastered the basics of tightrope-walking, we were on to somersaults. I sprang across the floor of the dusty courtyard. Jacques taught me the curvet, where I threw my body backwards while my hands, which were hardening like my feet, hit the floor and I flipped myself through a back somersault.

I showed him hand-walking. He shrugged and flung himself into an Arab somersault, cartwheeling across the courtyard before flipping himself through the air head over heels, and landing with a tiny puff of dust on both feet. "Show off!" I said, grinning.

The secret to somersaulting is to relax, your mind and body. It was the only time Jacques did relax. When we weren't somersaulting or tightroping, as I liked to call it, it was as if he shut himself down, retreated behind his fringe and glared at the world.

Sometimes it felt as if he didn't want me around at all. After one day when he'd been particularly sullen, grunting answers to questions or ignoring them altogether, I went to school instead of the courtyard, pinching my cheeks on the way there to make myself look as ill as I could.

When I came out he was waiting.

"Oh, hello," I said. The rest of the class filed past looking down on the French boy and sniffing at his tattered shorts and bare feet. "Tsk," said Primrose.

"Come," said Jacques when the girls had gone. I said nothing. I was still cross with him. He led me down to the lower part of the fort, to where the cavalry's horses and the bullocks and camels lived.

He nodded to the bored, sweaty soldier leaning against the stable door. Inside the stable was dark and nicely cool compared to the stifling heat outside. A couple of horses poked their heads out of stalls. The smell of horse and hay was strong.

"Here," said Jacques, pointing to the end stalls.

Unlike the other stalls, the two at the end had wooden spikes nailed to the top of their doors and a thick piece of wood angled against them to keep them secured.

I stood on tiptoes and peered through the spikes of the door on the right. It was gloomy down this end of the stable and all I could make out was a dark shape lying on a bed of hay.

"Not that one – that's Captain Brown's bear cub. He brought him all the way from the Afghan mountains. Here..."

I crossed to the left-hand side and looked through another set of spikes at another dark shape, this one larger. Jacques let out a low whistle and a head looked up from the hay.

"Bonjour, Tonton," said Jacques. "Comment allez vous?"

Jacques' voice was bright. I'd never heard him sound like that. It could be because he was speaking his first language but I was sure the answer lay on the other side of the stall door.

A strange noise was coming from the stall, as if Tonton had a sore throat and needed to gargle to ease the pain.

"Is Tonton not well?"

"Non, non, non… Tonton is pleased to see us. That noise, that is the noise she makes when she is 'appy – she is glad we 'ave come to see her.

Jacques opened the door and stepped into the stall. "Come, stay close to me – she must learn your smell and see you are no threat… to her or me."

"She protects you?"

"Of course – she would attack anyone who attacked me – and I look after her."

The tiger rose and stretched, looking like an oversized cat. She yawned, showing off a wide mouth and ever-so-sharp teeth. Imagine having to put your head in there! A trickle of fear ran down my back. Now that Tonton was on her feet the size and strength of the beast was clear to see even in the half-light of the stable.

She strolled towards us, soundless on her great paws, still making the gargling sound. Jacques took her head in his hands and rubbed behind her ears. Tonton looked like she was smiling, then with a deep grunt that made me start, she dropped to the ground and rolled on to her back, front legs tucked towards her chin.

Her white tummy, zigzagged by the dark lines of her markings, shone in the gloom. Jacques bent on one knee and started stroking her stomach. Tonton's head tipped back in pleasure as she gargled happily.

"Come," said Jacques, "you do it."

Tonton raised her head as I knelt down. Carefully, ever so carefully, I reached out a hand and touched the white fur. It felt wiry but one rub exposed the softness of the coat beneath.

"Each tiger has their own markings – every single one is different."

"Aaaaarrrrggggggghhh," gargled Tonton as I ran

my hand up and down her stomach. She tipped her head back again, resting it on the floor. I had passed the tiger tickle test.

A visit to Tonton became part of our daily routine. Either we would go down to the stables after practice and lie on the straw stroking her tummy, or Jacques would be waiting round the corner from the school room and together we would run away from the rest of my class, who were desperate to know where I went off to with the strange circus boy.

He still didn't talk much. Most of our time together passed in silence, a necessary silence when he was watching me on the tightrope or instructing me in a growing repertoire of flips and tricks and somersaults. Afterwards we would sit together, on a good day sharing one of Private Coombe's oranges (you didn't think I would really give them all to Primrose did you?); on a not-so good-one listening to our tummies rumble (food was ever more tightly rationed).

Sometimes a silence can hang between people and you feel the need to speak. But it wasn't like that with Jacques. I like to chatter; I know people think I'm a chatterbox but what's wrong with that? What's wrong with wanting to talk, to ask questions, give opinions and best of all tell stories?

Yet I have never felt the need to fill the silence around Jacques, even if it did annoy me when he spoke to Tonton in French. One day I heard him mention Vette to the tiger – Tonton's ears pricked up, and so did mine. I was desperate to join in; I wanted to know what he said but bit my tongue.

"Owww," I said instead and the boy and the tiger looked at me.

That was the first time I noticed how thin Tonton was becoming. In the fort she was right at the bottom of the food chain – first came the governor, then the soldiers, then the civilians, then the horses, then the camels and bullocks and then Captain Brown's bear and then, and only then, Tonton. A circus tiger is not a priority in a siege.

Jacques tried to persuade Private Coombe to pinch

a chicken for Tonton, offering him the magician's chest in return. The jewelled chest was part of the circus paraphernalia crammed into the carriage Jacques and Vette had brought into the fort. But Private Coombe didn't need any magic in his life.

"I'd swing for it if they caught me, Master Jacques. I'll do what I can for your tiger 'cos she's a magnificent beast but I ain't hanging for her or nobody."

It was a week of firsts. Two days later I first spotted we were being spied on. I was upside down, walking on my hands across the courtyard as a warm-up to my toughest test yet. I was to attempt a somersault on the tightrope itself.

Out of the corner of my eye I caught a flash of white by the entrance to the passage. I sprang back to my feet. There was someone there. I raced over to the passage in time to hear the retreating slap of bare feet on the stone floor.

I gave chase, burst out of the passage and swung a quick look left, then right. There was no one there.

"Pah," I said. It was probably one my classmates, most likely one of the older Winter sisters. I didn't want them finding out what I was doing because as sure as the nights were hot and the days boiling they would tell, and word would get to Aunt Constance. And then… now that didn't bear thinking about.

I noticed an Indian boy squatting in a doorway. He wore the white uniform of the governor's servants.

"Has anyone come past?" I asked.

The boy looked up at me. His face was familiar. Where had I seen it? Never mind. I looked away, up and down the alleyway again. Nobody.

"Anybody?"

The boy shook his head.

"Bother," I said. I spun on my heel and marched back to the courtyard, where I decided I wasn't ready to try a somersault on the tightrope I wasn't in the mood. I threw myself down on the cushions.

Jacques watched and said nothing for a while. He sat down beside me.

"I'm hungry." I broke the silence, as I usually do.

"You can try tomorrow. You are good enough to do it."

"Am I? You think so? You really think so?"

Jacques shrugged. "I do not waste my words."

"What if that was someone from my class spying on us – I know what they're like. They have no lives of their own so they like interfering in others. I'll be stopped from coming here. Stopped from seeing you, and Tonton."

Jacques shrugged again.

"Oh for goodness sake, Jacques. You can't spend the rest of your life shrugging."

I stood up and glared at him; if he lifted those shoulders one more time I'd... why I'd...

"Why do you turn on other people when you are upset at something for yourself?"

Jacques' words cut me.

"So you don't care if I can't come here?"

If he shrugged this time, I'd be furious, raging... why I'd...

Then it hit me, smack across the cheek. You don't always see what's in front of you. I'd be torn apart if I couldn't come and see Jacques. I liked coming here because I wanted to be an acrobat and he was teaching me, but more than that – I liked being with *him*, liked having a friend, a real friend. Yes, that's what he was. I couldn't stop myself smiling. I absolutely wanted Jacques to be my friend.

The smile stayed put when he answered.

"Yes I would care but what will be will be." And he shrugged. "C'est la vie."

I dived for him but he was too quick. He rolled aside and I sunk into the mound of cushions, which just about muffled my giggles.

The next day should have been a school day. I decided not to go and made a string of further promises to Primrose I knew I couldn't keep – washing up for eternity. But after what Jacques said, I had to get back to the courtyard. If he believed in me, I wanted to show him he was right and I could throw a somersault on the tightrope without ending up in an untidy, moaning heap in the dust.

Jacques was on the tightrope when I arrived in the courtyard. I stood in the mouth of the passage and watched him. It looked easy, flipping backwards along the tightrope, feet to hands to feet to hands. Or rather he made it look easy. So easy anyone could do it. I touched the elephant-headed carving, for luck. Don't know why, it just seemed right.

I couldn't do it on my first attempt. I chickened out of it actually, settling for just – just! – walking across the tightrope (that seemed easy now). And I chickened out of my second go as well and this time lost my balance. I was good enough to land on my feet, feet hardened enough to deal with a fall. Without thinking I bent my knees on impact to limit the blow of the landing. See? Pretty good now.

"Allezzz huuuuup," said Jacques and clapped his hands. "Again."

I climbed back on, stretched my arms to find my balance and…

"There!" I yelled, pointed and lost my balance. This time I fell on my front.

The fall drove the breath from me but I wasn't going to let the spy get away a second time. Ignoring the pain, I scrambled back to my feet and ran for the passage.

With a puzzled Jacques close behind I burst out into the alleyway. Glanced left and right. Nobody. The Indian boy was there again in the doorway. He was breathing heavily.

"You!" I said and stood in front of him, hands on hips, face smeared with dirt.

"Who?" said Jacques, joining me.

"The spy," I said.

"The spy?"

"The spy?"

Jacques and the boy spoke at the same time. The boy stood up and faced me. He was a pinky finger taller than me. He too placed his hands on his hips, like he was mimicking me… teasing me.

I took a step back.

"Um, yes," I insisted. I pulled my shoulders back. I'd show him who was in charge. There was still three-quarters of a pinky finger between us. "This is the boy who's been spying on us, Jacques."

"Oh, I see," said the boy. "Now you notice me – when you decide I've done something wrong. You didn't see me yesterday did you, Missie Baba? Oh no, it couldn't have been me spying on you yesterday could it, because I'm just an Indian boy, just a servant, I'm nothing to you. I might as well be see-through."

He prodded a bony finger into my chest to mark each word of his final sentence. He was all long limbs, long legs, long arms and long fingers.

"I-*prod*-might-*prod*-as-*prod*-well-*prod*-be-*prod*-see-through-*prod*."

Gently, ever so gently, he replaced the finger with a palm and eased me aside.

"You British, pah… no wonder so many people want to kill you."

I stepped back and he set off down the alleyway.

I was lost for words. Which may very well have been a first.

"I'm not British." Jacques aimed his words after the retreating figure.

"You're all the same, *feringhi*."

The boy stopped and spun round. He raised his pointy finger again. "You don't belong here. You, your people, you come here to this land – our land – to take… take, take, take, you are ruining my land and you are ruining my people."

Are we? Father wouldn't have been doing that would he? I tried to listen carefully to what the boy was saying, but as I looked at him properly for the first time there was something familiar about his face. I'd definitely seem him somewhere…

"Ah, got it!" I exclaimed. "I recognise you – I know where I've seen you."

"Well I am honoured – so tell on me then, report me to your memsahib and come watch me whipped."

"No," I said. This was not going at all as I expected. Why was he so cross? "That's not what… you were in the Governor's rooms. You… you're the one who stuck his tongue out at me."

I turned to Jacques, smiling at the memory. "All

very proper it was, being allowed to meet His Most-Importantness the Great Governor, and he… him…" This time I pointed. "…he sticks his tongue out at me when everybody else is looking the other way."

I laughed. "That was funny."

The boy looked puzzled. "You made me laugh," I pointed out.

"I have to go," said the boy. He turned and walked up the alleyway.

"Wait… what's your name?"

"Pingali." The boy flung his name over his shoulder. "Pingali Rao."

"Well, Pingali Rao, come back and watch us… if you want…"

Pingali Rao walked on without giving any indication he'd heard my invitation. Maybe he thought I didn't mean it; after all he didn't seem that keen on the British. I hoped he would come because I didn't mean to be taking his country away. India was proving a confusing place to live.

"That's all right, isn't it Jacques?"

Jacques shrugged.

Just appearing was one of Pingali Rao's tricks. We would become used to it over the coming months but to begin with it surprised us every time. He was a surprising boy. One minute there was no Pingali Rao, next minute there he was. We never heard him coming.

"Oh, hello," I said. I was sitting on the ground in the shade of the walkway around the hidden courtyard. It was hot, even hotter than normal. Jacques had me practising hard.

"No mistakes… not a single mistake – I must have perfection," he said. He was always demanding more when we were practising. I enjoyed it when he was like this. It felt as if it was for real; we really were acrobats preparing for a show in the Big Top.

"Roll up, roll up for the Great Romanini and the Flying Scot," the ringmaster would roar, and the packed crowd would "oooh" and "aaah" as me and Jacques took flight over their heads. I liked to imagine it at night as I drifted towards sleep, trying to ignore Primrose's smelly feet twitching inches from my nose (mine were just as smelly if I'm being honest), while closing my eyes and seeing myself fly. Some nights Mother got in the way. "We miss you terribly, my wee darling," she'd say and I would wake with a start and sit up expecting her to be by my bed.

"You didn't tell me your name." Pingali sat down beside me. "May I?"

"Oh, yes, of course – you don't have to ask."

"Best to – you English have lots of rules and regulations for what people, especially Indian people, can and cannot do. And for an Indian it can be painful to get it wrong."

"I wouldn't do anything to you," I said, then added fiercely, "I'm not like them."

"Perhaps so," said Pingali "But I do not know that… here I bought you this."

He handed me a large green piece of fruit; in places

its skin had turned to gold and was smooth to the touch.

"What is it?"

"A mango," said Jacques, standing over us, his brow dotted with beads of sweat. "I'm Jacques." He stuck out his hand. Pingali looked at it, head cocked to one side. He stood up and shook it.

"Very pleased to make your acquaintance, Jacques."

I stood up too and thrust my hand out. "I'm Beatrice Spelling but I don't like being called Beatrice. Call me Bea."

Pingali shook my hand. "Well you can call me Pin then. I've always wanted someone to call me Pin."

He reached up and pulled a small knife from the curls of his uniform turban. He cut open the mango, sliced carefully around the stone and handed pieces to me and Jacques.

Grannie always said I'm a fussy eater. At home in Glen Laddich I liked my boiled egg for breakfast, my cheese piece to take with me for lunch somewhere up the glen if I was going exploring and finally for dinner something I knew. Grannie says I eat as if the dish needs to earn my trust. I've got better since I came to India. I'm trying new things. I touched the slice of mango with the tip of my tongue, then bit a slither off.

"Yummm," I said and filled my mouth with sweet fruit. The juice ran down my chin; I wiped it away with a dart of my hand.

"You do not eat like any British lady I have seen," said Pin.

I tried to reply but couldn't get any words past the mango. It was one of the best things I've ever tasted, absolutely forever and ever. Amen.

Pin beamed a smile at us. His enthusiasm was infectious, and his library of stories from his work in the governor's palace kept us chatting and laughing, sprawled on the cushions for the rest of the morning. He did an excellent impression of the governor. We forgot about our practice. Even Jacques laughed and when he did his face filled with the real Jacques – the Jacques I'd seen in the circus. I was worried a part of him might have gone with Vette and would never come back. But all of him was still there. Perhaps it was just a case of giving him time.

Pin enjoyed having an audience. He turned down my offer of a go on the tightrope.

"I have a head full of knowledge," he declared. "And I will not risk losing that by bumping it."

Instead he talked and talked, hands weaving and waving to decorate his tales, and he had many tales. Because his role meant he saw everything, and because he was a servant nobody saw him.

His job, I was bewildered to learn, was to turn pages. He stood behind the governor all day, and sometimes in the evening too; when the most important man finished reading a page, in a book or his official paperwork, Pin would lean forward and turn to the next one.

"Page turner?" I said, shaking my head. "You turn pages?"

"Yes," said Pin. "I have been doing this for five, no six, years I think."

"That's all you do?"

"All I do… I stand there for hour after hour, from the morning when he takes his breakfast right through to the evening when the sun has gone and he wants to read a little before his bed. Yes, that's what I do… I turn pages – that is my place in the governor's house."

"You must be bored silly."

Pin stared at me. He had large brown eyes that shone.

"Bored? I think bored is for rich people. I have my work and I have to do it. If not, I get whipped and then I will have no job and I will have to beg on the streets and I will not live very long on the streets. I must not go back to the streets."

"Oh," I said. I felt like a silly wee girl. I could feel my cheeks reddening.

Pin smiled at me again. "It is not your fault, Beatrice Spelling who likes to be called Bea. It is the way it is."

He paused for a moment, shook his head. "But it will not always be like this I think; this war will bring change."

"The mutiny you mean?"

"You British call it ghadr; we call it war."

"Are you a mutineer?"

"I am a servant, I am but a boy."

"That doesn't matter. Boys can do lots." It was Jacques' first contribution.

"I know a lot," replied Pin. That's what he was like, Pin. He said what he thought because he wasn't afraid of what he thought. And he did know a lot, an awful lot.

He'd filled those long years standing beside the governor's chair not by daydreaming or staring into space with a blank mind. Instead he filled his mind. First he learnt to read, risking a whipping by sneaking into the governor's children's rooms, listening to their bedtime stories and then taking their books when they were asleep. Borrowing them really. He would allow himself a few nights with each – the book had to be back in place before anyone knew it had gone – reading on and on by candlelight as the palace bell struck one, two, three, four.

When he could read to his satisfaction, he began stuffing himself full of knowledge; Pin read and read until his head was bursting. He read everything the governor did. So it was English books only and he was fond of many of them because, as Pin pointed out, a good story is a good story whether it happens in London or Agra.

Charles Dickens was his favourite – he enjoyed it when the governor relaxed in the evening with a Dickens book. The governor had just finished *Oliver Twist*, a story Pin enjoyed enormously – the Artful Dodger was his favourite character in all the English books he'd ever read. "That Mr Dickens knows very well about poor children," he said. "The things you have to do to survive."

It wasn't just books Pin read. He saw all the official papers, the papers of government, and so, after the governor, Pin was the second-best informed person in Agra. Actually if you take into account that Pin, unlike the governor, also spoke to Indian people in the fort and around the city, then he was quite possibly *the* best informed person in Agra. A servant who knew more than his master.

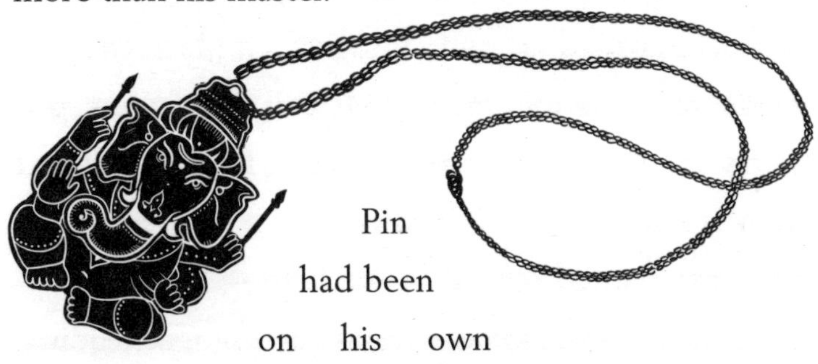

Pin had been on his own for a long time. His beginnings were as mysterious as any legend. "I wonder," he told us, "who I am, but not everything has an explanation. Instead I have Ganesha with me always to guide me on my journey."

He pointed at the elephant-head carving and with his other hand pulled a necklace from beneath his top. At its end hung a small wooden carving. It was roughly done, but was the same: the head of an elephant, this one with a full trunk, and the body of a roly-poly human beneath.

"Oh!" I said.

"This was with me when I was found, wrapped in a red and blue sari and left on the doorstep of a sweet shop," explained Pin.

He'd been discovered in the city by some children, whose shouts attracted an old servant returning to the fort. The old man took the abandoned baby, with the necklace wound around one wrist, and brought him to the fort. "He told me I gurgled all the way up, as if I was telling him something, a story. Perhaps how I'd come to be left on a doorstep.

"They named me in the kitchens – Pingali Rao – Pingali after a great poet the old man enjoyed reading. Rao, well, Rao because one of the cooks thought a short name was best because it saved time and there is never enough time.

"I called the old man my grandfather and he told me stories in return for the one I told him on that first day."

In the evenings the old man would take Pin on his lap and carry him away on a journey. He told

Pin of Hamza and his quest to overcome the evil Zumurrud Shah amid sorcerers, dragons and flying carpets – "Everyone hopes for a flying carpet in our stories," Pin informed us. Or the long, long tale of Ravana, the terrible many-headed demon king, and how his army of demons was defeated by Lord Rana himself.

To me India was beginning to sound a lot like Scotland – there were stories and spirits everywhere and in everything, the hills, the plains, the glens, the forests, the land, the very rocks and trees, the water, the heavens above and the underworld below. Grannie used to tell me of Cailleach Bheur, the fearsome goddess of winter, who washes her hair in the sea and makes a deadly whirlpool. Here, in the very waters of the Jumna, Pin told us, there once lived Kaliya, a naga, half-human, half-serpent, who made the water froth with his poison. Nothing could live in the river and only one lonely kadamba tree stood on its banks. Until Krishna came and danced on Kaliya's serpent head and banished him from the river so its waters could bring life once more.

"I know many, many stories..." said Pin, "apart from the beginning of mine."

He had no memory before the fort. The odd thing was nobody could tell him whether he was an orphan for certain because nobody knew anything about his parents. One day, he promised himself, he would leave the fort, run away from the governor, and find who he really was. "Perhaps my mother is a Mughal princess who fell on hard times," he said. "My father a warrior…"

"I'm an orphan," I said abruptly, interrupting him. It sounded odd – I'd never said it aloud before. Pin leaned his head to one side and looked at me.

"That is sad," he said.

"Sometimes it is," I said and he reached out a hand and touched my arm.

One morning when he was six or maybe seven or even eight (nobody could tell him how old he was – Pin was a boy without a birthday), he'd been taken from the kitchens and marched up to the governor's office. By that afternoon he was turning pages and carrying books and papers. And here he was six or so years later, a deal taller, a great deal smarter, still turning pages.

"Why are you not turning pages today?" Jacques

eyed Pin warily, as if he might not be who he said he was.

"Because the governor is out... he's gone on an inspection tour. There is no rebel army outside Agra, it is still some miles off, so the governor has gone to take a look around, see the damage to the city."

"So are we not in a siege anymore?"

"Yes and no – outside the fort it is dangerous, danger everywhere for you British, much chaos, lots of people who want to cut your heads off..."

He grinned at me. I didn't care much for the prospect of losing my head but I also didn't want Pin to know it bothered me. I need to keep up appearances, as Miss Goodenough liked to say.

"You are safe in here – the Indian soldiers do not have enough cannon to knock down the walls, but there is nowhere else you can go until the British soldiers arrive from Lucknow, so in that way you are under siege."

"When will that be – the soldiers arriving?"

Pin raised his hands, palms up. "One month, six months, one year... it is difficult to say for certain."

"But the food... it's already pretty terrible. We'll run out, won't we?"

I licked my lips, searching for any last taste of mango.

"That is very possible in the circumstances," said Pin. "Yes, one day the food will run out and then... and then, well, I don't know what happens in this story."

"Non… non, non, NON."

Jacques kicked the stable door in anger. It swung open and he ran inside, disappearing into the gloom.

I looked at Private Coombe who was staring after Jacques, shaking his head. He turned to me.

"It's not my fault, Miss, I said it's not fair, but they said it's an order and an order's an order. Same for the bear – Captain Brown's furious so he is."

He put his hands out, pleading. "You see in the army if you don't obey an order I'd be whipped and…"

"What order?"

"It's the food see, Miss… it's getting ever so low. The horses are getting very little and we need them in case of battle, see, and the camels and bullocks, well, they pull the cannons so they have to be fed…"

"Which leaves Tonton."

"Exactly, Miss."

"But she doesn't eat what horses eat."

Private Coombe shrugged. "But she eats what people eat, meat and that, and that's running ever so short… so I've been told… been ordered…"

"To kill Tonton… so the soldiers can eat her… NO!"

"No, no, Miss – the order is not to spare any food for the tiger anymore."

"Oh, I… but that will kill her…"

Private Coombe looked down at his feet.

"Jacques!" I ran down the line of stalls until I reached Tonton's. Jacques was already inside. He had Tonton's head on his lap and was stroking her flank. I could make out the jagged interruptions of her ribs poking through her once shiny coat. She was getting thinner and thinner.

"I'll find Pin – he'll have an answer."

I wish I had an answer myself. I had one idea – we would steal a cooked chicken from the big fort kitchen. Quite how we would do that I wasn't sure, and what we would do after one chicken I had no idea. We couldn't keep stealing chickens to feed a ravenous tiger. And there was no end to the siege in sight.

Pin would have an answer, for sure. He'd been spending all his precious free moments with us in the courtyard. He'd encourage us when we were tightroping, pretending he was the ringmaster. He had Jacques describe every detail of a ringmaster's role. Then made up his own. Words came easily to him. He was like a talking book.

Pin would know what to do. I had a feeling about that, and I always say you have to act on your feelings.

As I ran up to the governor's palace, I was surprised to feel anger, real red hot fury, bubbling inside me. This time I let it come to the boil. Poor Jacques – this war was nothing to do with him. The Indians were not fighting against what the French had done, it was about what us British had done. And Jacques was trapped in the middle of it. It had already cost him his livelihood with the destruction of the circus and the likely death of all those circus people he lived and worked with.

Then, hardest of all, it had cost him the life of his

precious sister, poor Vette, and now they wanted to take away the last thing keeping him going. Without Tonton, I feared, Jacques would give up, give up on everything, even life itself.

"Oi, where d'you think you're going?"

The sentry was so startled by my sudden appearance – I am a quick runner – he made no move to stop me. I hurried through the vast hallway and leaned into the tall double doors that led into the governor's office.

The governor leapt up from his desk, scrabbling for the pistol he kept beside his inkwell for just such a moment, and beside him Theophilus Campbell actually squawked in alarm. But instead of a mob of murderous mutineers bursting through the doors, they were instead confronted by me, a thin, red-headed, and hot-headed, girl of nearly 13.

"Beatrice… what the blazes…"

"Haud yer wheest, Uncle Theo…" It was out before I could stop it – Grannie's favourite phrase when she'd had enough – and that was only the beginning. I boiled over, hissing and steaming. I turned my furious attention to the governor.

"How dare you starve poor Tonton, how dare you order her not to be fed, why do you decide who should live and who should die? You're a horrid man who just sits up here all day ordering this or that, eating your food – does your tummy rumble with hunger at night when you lie in your bed? Of course you will have a big, normal bed won't you... and a bath, I'm sure you don't have to squat in a barrel after goodness knows how many people have been in before you trying to make yourself clean. All because you're too scared to go out and fight, too scared to..."

It was the second "too scared" that snapped the governor out of it. He had sat there in open-mouthed astonishment in the face of my verbal battering, but being called "scared" by a child, and a girl to boot, was the final straw (precisely because I was right, and I knew I was right because that's what Pin had told me).

"Whaaaaaattt!" roared the governor. "Who is this damned girl... get her out of here Campbell, get her out... she should be horsewhipped and I'd do it myself if I wasn't a very busy and very important man. Out... OUT!"

Uncle Theo came bustling round the desk to confront me. I glanced round him and nodded at Pin, who was standing stock still behind the governor's chair – I'd avoided looking at him until now because I didn't want to run the slightest risk of anyone spotting a connection between us.

Pin would understand and he would come and find us as soon as he could.

"Right, you," said Uncle Theo, raising his hand as he approached. I could see the anger in his face. I didn't wait to see what he was going to do with his hand. I turned and ran and once again the sentry didn't lay a finger on me. He was too busy thinking about the story he'd have to tell when he got back to the barracks, how this wild barefooted girl with long red hair and flaming eyes had torn strips off the governor and Cautious Campbell as well.

I was too quick for Uncle Theo.

"Get back here now… or you will be whipped, by God you will be thrashed, girl."

I ignored his shouts, tore across the square in front of the palace and dived into the alleyways that led off it. It did not take long to make the turning to the hidden courtyard. I stopped running. My chest was heaving. I wiped sweat off my brow. It was so hot, no wonder my temper had boiled over. I smiled grimly; yes I'd been cross but it had also been an act. Well, it had begun as an act. It didn't need much to light the fire. Barging in was the only way to get into the governor's office – he would never have agreed to see a girl – and the only way to get our urgent message to Pin.

I glanced up and down the alley. All clear – we had to stay hidden because we were in big trouble. We were all for the whip if we were discovered. Not that I cared a jot at that moment. It felt cooler in the passage and I could feel my heartbeat beginning to slow. I took deep breaths, but even under here out of the sun the air was full of dust. I coughed.

"Who's there?"

"It's me."

Jacques was standing at the end of the passage, clutching a piece of wood like it was a club. I threw my arms around him, pinning his to his sides. I hugged him, then let go, dropping my arms to my side.

"Sorry," I said. "Don't know why I did that."

Jacques sat down on the cushions. He leaned back and closed his eyes, putting his hands over them as well.

"Pin will have an idea – he knows everything, remember."

"No one knows everything," muttered Jacques.

"I was being silly, Jacques. Come on, we'll think of something between us – you'll see, and we'll save Tonton."

We sat in silence after that, waiting for Pin. Jacques didn't want to talk so after a bit I climbed on to the tightrope. Because it required absolute concentration I thought it would be a good way to empty my mind of our troubles, at least for a minute or two. I fell off halfway across, twisting my ankle, the first time in ages I'd taken a tumble.

I sat in the courtyard rubbing my ankle. I closed my eyes and wished I was back home; Grannie calling me out of the loch for lunch, goose bumps breaking out across my shoulders as I tore across the soft grass and up to the house.

"What's the matter, Bea?"

Pin put out a hand and pulled me up. I brushed the dust off my knees. I'm sick of dust, dust, dust. I noticed he had a red mark on his face. "What's that?"

"Oh, nothing," he said, dropping himself on to the cushions next to Jacques. "Just where the governor slapped me before he had me thrown out of the palace."

"Pin! Why? What did you do?"

"I did nothing – it's what you did."

He looked up at me.

"Me?"

"Yes, you see you made a fool of the governor in front of soldiers and servants. So when you got away he needed to turn on someone, so he turned on me. Because that's what people like him do. I am never to go back there."

"Oh, Pin… I… I…"

"So now I have nowhere to sleep, nowhere to eat."

I gulped. Me and my big mouth, acting on my feelings. Leaping without looking. Always the same. Stupid Bea.

"Sorry," I whispered. "I thought it was a good idea."

"Hey," said Pin and shimmied along the cushions to create space for me. "It's what Ganesha has planned for me – he will look after me. Ganesha will guide you – those were Grandfather's last words to me."

He pulled out his necklace and wrapped his hand around the elephant head. It disappeared into his palm.

"So who is Ganesha? I keep hearing and seeing him but I don't…"

"You don't know Ganesha?"

The way he said it I felt silly, as if I should know Ganesha.

"Everyone knows Ganesha."

"Well, I don't..." It came out as a snap.

"I will tell you then as Grandfather told me..."

"Later," I said. I felt embarrassed about snapping and snappy about being embarrassed.

"Good idea," said Pin. "It's not a story to be rushed."

"Anyway what happened with the governor?" Jacques's change of subject was just right.

"Ha! Very funny. I wanted to laugh out loud. And I was going to leave anyway – you can't spend your life turning pages in another man's book, can you?"

"Were you really going to leave?" A surge of relief lifted me as I sat down beside him.

"Well of course – we need to get Tonton out don't we? Can't have the Queen of the Jungle starved to death by the British can we? I've seen the order signed by the governor, no more food for the tiger or the bear – had time to think about it..."

"Ahhh-haaa," I yelped and clapped my hands together. "See, Jacques – told you Pin would have a plan. Because..."

I stood up and adopted my best ringmaster pose. "Pin the Planner knows everything. Prepare to be marvelled by the King of Knowledge, the Emperor of… er, the Emperor of something very clever."

This was a proper tunnel. Proper in that it was dark, not very wide, not very high, and scary. There would be spiders. Big spiders with hairy legs and huge webs.

Pin, Jacques and Tonton were little more than shapes ahead of me. I swallowed and quickened my pace to keep up with them, doing my best to ignore the scuttling sounds of mice and who knows what else. I dearly hoped they weren't rats. Or, deep breath, scorpions.

We were somewhere underneath the fort, far underneath and if Pin really did know what he was doing (and I really hoped he did because getting lost down here didn't bear thinking about), we'd emerge in the city.

"In the city? In Agra?"

"Yes," said Pin.

He'd pinched the idea from one of the stories his grandfather told him. Pin said it was one of the oldest tales ever told, and one of the longest. It took his grandfather nearly a year to tell it from start to finish.

"Don't worry, I will give you only a few verses for now," said Pin. He had a way of talking that suited stories, a voice that rose and fell, hurried and strolled. It was about two families, each wanted to rule the land. One was the Pandavas. One day their palace was attacked by their deadly enemies the Kauravas and set on fire. The Pandavas appeared doomed to a terrible death, but they had a secret way out: a tunnel beneath their palace.

They hurried out the tunnel and disguised themselves as humble peasants, going from village to village begging food until they were out of danger.

"We're going to beg?"

He could tell I wasn't at all sure about his plan. As a servant, he'd spent so long watching others he could read people like one of his favourite books.

"We can't get Tonton to the jungle unless we leave here and we can't leave here without going through

Agra and if we don't leave here, Tonton will die. And as for the rest of us... well. We're not exactly welcome here are we? I have no work, no place to sleep, no food, no drink, no future in Agra... Jacques and Tonton are an unwanted burden on the British, they do not care about them and you... you Beatrice Spelling face the thrashing of your life according to the promise I heard from your uncle."

I swallowed. "What about out there? There are people who will kill me and kill Jacques."

We were caught between the devil and the deep blue sea.

"I've thought of that – you'll go in disguise."

"Disguise? As what? And what are you going to disguise a tiger as?"

"Look, Bea you're scared – I see that and it's all right to be scared because..."

"I am NOT scared," I said and raised my foot to stamp in order to emphasise the point. I changed my mind halfway through – I didn't want to act the spoilt child. So instead I hovered on one leg. Jacques chuckled.

"I'm not," I insisted, feeling my cheeks flush with anger. I put my foot down.

"Bea, I'm going with Pin because I must save Tonton. I would like you to come as well."

"What about afterwards... after we've found the jungle and set Tonton free, what then?"

I knew Jacques would shrug in response. He answered too.

"Pin will think of something."

I could hear the scuffle of the boys' footsteps ahead of me in the tunnel. I wondered what Aunt Constance's reaction would be when I didn't turn up tonight or tomorrow or the next day. A tut and a tsk and on with the day. They wouldn't miss me.

The others had stopped. Tonton coughed, a deep grunt; her tail was high. It meant she was on alert.

"Shhh," hushed Pin.

We waited, Jacques scratching behind Tonton's ears. The tiger lay down. She was weak, her strength ebbing away. Pin believed it would only take a few days to reach the jungle if luck was on our side. Given the state Tonton was in, that was probably as long as we had, yet already we were delayed and we weren't even out of the tunnels.

There was a warren beneath the fort – all sorts of

ways in and out. "Most servants know a way in and out," explained Pin. The tunnels had been there ever since the fort was built 300 years before, some known by the British, many not, and many others simply forgotten by everyone.

"All clear," said Pin. He led us out of the tunnel, which sloped upwards and emerged in the cellar of a house. Tonton padded silently up the stairs with Jacques. The house was deserted.

"Wait here," said Pin and before either of us could say "Why? Where are you going?" he was gone.

Jacques and I crouched either side of Tonton, each draping an arm around her, both to comfort her and seek comfort from her. After all, who doesn't feel safer for having a tiger on their side?

Jacques hummed a tune and Tonton pushed her head against him. It always amazed me how close the tiger and Jacques were. It also made me a little jealous – I do have green eyes after all. I wished I could have that special bond with a tiger like Tonton. I sighed and stood up.

I peered through the front door of the house but all was black outside. Distant sounds drifted in, the noises of a city in distress, shouts, a gunshot. I could smell burning. I crouched down again next to Tonton. How would Jacques bear to part with his tiger? Maybe he wouldn't, maybe he would stay in the jungle with her. Maybe I could as well, and Pin. Was that possible? In story books it was. In Pin's stories I'm sure it would be.

"Here, try these on."

Pin was back, slipping through the door without a sound. He dropped a bundle of clothes on a table.

"Your disguise," he added. "Quick – we must be out of the city by daybreak. When you're dressed, bring Tonton out, I've something for her as well."

I picked out a long piece of colourful cloth, green and gold with zigzagged lines across it, and draped it around me and over my head as I'd seen the Indian women do.

"No, no," said Pin. "You must take your English clothes off, your dress – you cannot keep it if the disguise is to work."

I looked at him doubtfully.

Pin gestured out the door. "You were right when you said there are men out there who want to kill you. They have already killed women and, yes, children.

This is not one of your childish English games, like in those stories the governor reads to his children. They will cut you down.

"No, no…" he shook his head at me. "You must have a proper disguise… if you give us away we will all be caught and I will suffer the same fate for helping you – we will all die."

I swallowed. I glanced back at the stairs to the cellar, where the tunnel led back to the fort, the narrow bed, Primrose's feet in my face and in the morning a thrashing from Uncle Theo. And then what? I would not be allowed to go off anywhere. I'd be under the constant watch of Aunt Constance. Even when the siege ended, I would be stuck right back in the dreary life of the bungalow, school, bungalow, school, and when I left school Aunt Constance and Uncle Theo would probably make me marry some cavalry officer who loved his horse more than me, and I would never ever get to see what was going on in the world outside. I would be left to wonder forever.

I wonder what happened to the man with the snake? Perhaps when the siege started the snake got such a fright it ate the man…

Bea – concentrate. Think where you are, think

what you're leaving behind. A thrashing and a life of nothingness with more thrashings the minute you step out of line, sucking every last drop of colour from your life. A grey life. If that happened, I might as well be dead.

"Turn around," I instructed Pin and Jacques. I threw my dress in the corner and tried to make myself into an Indian.

"Here," said Pin when I was done, and, with a tug here and tuck there, put the finishing touches to my disguise.

I quite liked it – I wish I could have seen myself in a mirror. I wore a loose pair of dark cotton trousers and a baggy white cotton top with the green and gold sari wrapped around me and extending to cover my head. I felt at once cooler and freer than tied up in a dress. The sandals Pin found were too big. That didn't matter, I was happy barefoot.

"And you keep this bit draped across your face when we're on the road," said Pin.

He ran an eye over Jacques' costume and nodded. With his dark skin and dark hair Jacques looked every inch the Indian boy.

Pin's surprise was he'd even found some food,

mostly for Tonton, which the tiger wolfed down in a matter of moments.

There was one more surprise. "Hold out your hands..."

We did as told and he placed a wee white sticky bun in each of our hands.

I eyed it suspiciously. "What is it?"

"Modak," said Pin. "They're a bit old, but beggars can't be choosers – the Pandavas would tell you that. Eat... they're a little stale, but still nice, sweet – from Ghantawallah's, the best sweet shop in Agra. It's no longer open but I know a back door. We take it to mark the beginning of our great journey. I've kept one for Ganesha as well, so he'll come with us."

Pin lent down and placed one in the doorway. On the top right-hand corner of the doorframe was a small carving of the elephant-headed god. Pin knelt and muttered something I couldn't make out.

"Eat," he said, standing up again. I took a bite and my mouth filled with a sticky sweetness. "If you do not know Ganesha, you cannot know life, you cannot achieve anything. Grandfather taught me. Ganesha will clear our path if we are good to him – so I leave him a treat because there is nothing Ganesha loves more than sweets."

"Really?"

"Absolutely – why do you think he has such a large tummy…" Pin laughed. "And he needs a cobra as a belt to keep his tummy in. Look…" He pointed to the carving. I stood on tiptoes and studied it. Sure enough there was a snake sketched around his middle. I licked my lips, savouring the taste of the modak.

"He's with us," said Pin with a nod of satisfaction. "Now we go."

By dawn we'd left the city behind. As the sun peeked over the horizon – we were heading east – Pin hurried us off the road and into a thicket of trees. Vines and vegetation tangled between the trees. "Banyans," said Pin. "Some call it the strangler tree because it takes over others." He hacked a path with an ugly looking machete. He'd changed too; he no longer wore the uniform and turban of the governor's servants. He wore a loose blue and white robe and an everyday turban, bundled and tucked around his head. Out here he seemed more grown-up, more serious. Then again, he was trying to keep us alive.

"We'll hide here for the next couple of hours – the early morning and evening is when the roads are busiest, more chance of people taking an interest in us. We'll walk around midday – the sun will be at its hottest but the road its quietest. Then we'll hide up again and walk through the night."

"We can't walk at midday," I pointed out, "we'll boil – Private Coombe told me if you leave a sword out in the sun it becomes too hot to use. It will boil our heads."

Pin shook his head. "For *feringhi* soldiers maybe…" He lifted up a large water bottle hung over his shoulder. "With plenty of this we can do it."

We saw no one when we set out at noon, judging the time by when the blazing sun sat overhead. A weary haze hung on the horizon as we trudged along the road. The soil was red in the fields on either side, like they'd been bled dry. I looked at Pin's back – he was leading the way. It wasn't only Tonton's life that depended on him: it was all of ours.

After an hour we reached a village, or what was left of a village. None of the houses had roofs and most of their remaining walls were black with soot, painful shapes violently made. Bad things had happened here. There was a peculiar smell, sweet, but a sweetness that made you feel sick. I retched and Pin handed me the water vessel. A fat vulture sat hunched on one of the walls and watched us pass. Above our heads, two more circled, wings spread wide, slow and steady. I dreaded to think what might be behind the wall.

We managed another couple of hours plodding beneath the sun's merciless glare, our pace getting slower and slower, our heads bent lower and lower.

"We stop there," said Jacques at last. "This is madness."

Even Pin didn't have the strength to speak. He nodded and we trudged over to a tangle of trees behind a short stone wall that began nowhere and ended nowhere. We pushed into the shadiest spot, where the trees stooped and leaned in to provide a green roof above a small grass clearing.

A head appeared in the grass, then another. Tonton

let out a low growl. The heads turned into bodies, two men, each brandished a sword.

"Oh no," muttered Pin. I tried to swallow but my throat was too dry. The men raised their swords and barked something in a language I couldn't understand. Tonton growled again, this time louder and longer. Her ears flattened on her head, her eyes widened, menace prowled from every pore.

The men spotted the tiger and froze. Jacques whispered something to Tonton and the tiger stepped slowly forward, never taking her eyes from the nearest man.

"Ggggrrrrggghhhhh," snarled Tonton, still far below full volume (a tiger's roar carries for three miles) but louder than her first warning growls.

A rough translation from tigerese would be something like "I suggest you turn around and run as fast as you can before I rip you to shreds." The men agreed. One dropped his sword. Both ran. As fast as they could. We listened to their progress through the undergrowth, then silence fell. I bent to pick up the discarded sword and followed.

"Bea, wait," said Jacques.

"Going to make sure they've gone," I replied and marched off. I'm not here to hide behind the two boys. That's not how I do things.

I watched the men reach the road and hurry off, heading in the direction of the ruined village. They flung occasional glances over their shoulders but kept on running. They would not be back. I raised the sword and waved it after them. It was heavier than it looked.

"Who were they?" I asked when I returned to the clearing. Tonton was pacing around, exploring our new surroundings.

"Don't know," said Pin. "Gujars or Jats perhaps – countryside bandits out for themselves, looking for easy meat."

He shook his head. "It's difficult to know enemies and friends. So many are squabbling over the land, some who want to rob and take, others want what is theirs, some are good, wanting to protect their village, some are bad."

Pin looked at me. "But they do have one thing in common..."

He pointed one of his long fingers. "You... you British, we want rid of you. Leave us to work our own land. Leave us to read our own books. Everyone wants you gone."

"It's nothing to do with me," I said. Well, it wasn't was it? I thought of the village, the homes destroyed. What had happened to the children who lived there, the girls like me, boys like Pin and Jacques, boys like Baby George? Was this all Father's fault, Primrose's father's fault, Euphemia's father's fault, the fault of all the fathers of all the girls in my class? It couldn't be. Could it be?

"Who did that, to that village?"

"Don't know, your soldiers probably, they destroy everything in their path, making orphans everywhere… could also have been bandits, could even have been the rani. They say the rani's men have been seen close to Agra. They might have had a battle here with the British."

"The rani? Who's he?"

"She – the rani's a she. Named for a goddess. I have never seen her but I've heard stories, many stories. The rani of Jhansi, she leads an army, leads it herself into battle – they say she carries a sword in each hand and the reins of her horse in her mouth. Once she rode over 100 miles in one day and one night.

She rides like the wind. They say she wrestles a man before breakfast, can lift a man, fights like a man... I think she's like your Robin Hood, she takes from the rich and gives to the poor."

"She burnt down a village? That doesn't sound like Robin Hood!"

"If she did, she would have had good reason." Pin hurled his words at me. "You wouldn't understand. You don't understand anything."

"No I don't." I hurled them back. "I don't understand this place. I didn't want to come to your stupid land anyway. I don't know why my parents came to your stupid land. I understand my home and I want to go back there."

"Well, off you go," said Pin. He flung an arm in the direction he thought I should go.

"Mes enfants, non, non, non."

Jacques stepped between us. I shot Pin the fiercest glare I could. He scowled back at me.

"You are acting like two children."

"We are two children," I said, keeping my stare fixed on Pin.

"Two spoilt children – that's what you are being like. It is like Rose is here."

"Who's Rose?"

"That nose-in-the-air cousin you come out of school with."

"You mean Primrose."

"That's what I said."

"No it wasn't."

"Yes it was."

"No it... oh this is stupid." I didn't know which boy to glare at. So I turned my back on them both.

"ARRRGGGGHHHH!" I yelled. I needed to let it out.

Pin chuckled. I spun round. Jacques was grinning.

"You are like our own rani," said Pin, and sat down in the waist-high grass. He took a long drink of water and handed the flask to me.

"Here's one thing you have to know about my land – if you don't drink plenty, you will die."

I took the flask and sat down beside him. I was tired. Jacques whistled and Tonton ambled over; they lay down together. Jacques rested his head on Tonton's neck and closed his eyes.

I lay down on my side facing Pin. "Tell me about your land then."

He lay on his back and gazed up at the canopy. "One day I will tell you all about the greatness of it, the beauty that is everywhere, the smell after the rains when the earth comes alive, everything is in bloom and we forget the summer winds, winds so hot they make your very brain feel on fire. The devil's breath we call it.

"There are so many stories I could tell you, ancient, ancient tales… let me see… yes, there are enough legends about Ganesha alone to fill the thickest book you have ever seen, more than all your William Shakespeare's words put together and doubled and trebled.

"Hmmm, so…. Yes, once upon a time Ganesha's mother, the goddess Parvati, was making extra-special sweets for Ganesha and his brother Shanda. And you know how children are when they're waiting for sweets… you're so excited you think you're going to burst, and if Ganesha's tummy burst… Wow! That would be a lot of mess to clear up… so Parvati said to her boys, before you get any sweets you must go around the whole world, the whole universe…"

Pin waved his arms in a large circle. "And the first one to do so will get the best modak. So Shanda races off but Ganesha stands there and first of all he thinks. Then he walks around his mother and then he walks around Shiva, his father. And Parvati smiled the smile I expect only a mother can give her child and Ganesha had won the sweets.

"You see Ganesha is both clever and funny. If you can make someone happy then, yes, that is the greatest of gifts, isn't it Bea? Bea… Bea?"

"Huuummm," I said. My eyes were shut. I was on the edge of sleep, where words begin to lose meaning. I opened my eyes briefly and directed a smile his way.

"Happy," I mumbled – it felt an effort to move my jaw to let the words out. "Clever Pin will make us live happy ever after." Then I slept.

It took longer than Pin expected to reach the jungle. The heat beat down by day, stealing every last ounce of everything from you, even the ability to think. My head became empty. Night-time was a blessed relief but not for long because then we started to think again and as we hurried along through the dark, eyes and ears straining for any sign of trouble, the barking of jackals and unseen sounds of the night relit the fear in our bellies. Fear was all we had in our bellies – even Ganesha's great big tummy would have dwindled if he'd been with us. Day and night tummies rumbled and heads spun. Tonton seemed to become thinner before our eyes. "A horse, a horse, my kingdom for a horse," muttered Pin. I worried he was going mad.

A couple of times in the dawn's early light we saw

red coats approaching and leapt for cover. Another time we were lucky. Pin had sent Jacques up a tamarind tree to throw down some fruit. Jacques was climbing up when he gave a yell and pointed along the road.

"Soldiers!"

He scrambled down and we raced for the cover of a ruined house. We tucked ourselves behind the walls and listened to the tread of marching boots as the soldiers tramped past. Rebels and the British both wore red coats so it was impossible to tell from a distance whose side they might be on. Besides both were best avoided – rebels would certainly kill Jacques and me. The British would take us back to Agra, and certainly hang Pin from the nearest tree. Both sides would kill Tonton.

Everything was broken, burnt, destroyed, like the sun had fallen from the sky and set fire to the land. As we crept through an abandoned village, I saw what looked like a row of bodies. I turned the other way as we passed – I didn't want to see what had happened to them.

Seeing so much that was so awful: a burning house, vultures tugging at slaughtered animals, once even three men hanging from the branches of tree, a little bit more of me became certain we were not going to make it. I would have given up but didn't have the energy to argue with Pin when he kept us going.

And then, just as I became convinced we were on the road to nowhere, there it was. As the sun rose we crested a hill and Pin stopped and threw up an arm. In the distance beneath us the land changed from reddish brown to every shade of green.

"When the Pandavas were thrown out of their home and banished," declared Pin, sweeping a hand across the horizon, "they turned a barren land into a paradise and I think we've found it."

"Fingers crossed," I said. I squeezed mine tight and wondered how long it would take to turn a barren land into a paradise. "They must have worked like Trojans."

We stood in a row, Tonton's head peering between me and Jacques, and looked down on the jungle. Tonton raised her head and sniffed the air.

"That's going to be your home, Tonton," said Jacques, rubbing the white spot on the back of her left ear.

We decided not to rest up with the arrival of the

new day. Instead we took a good look around from the top of the hill, and seeing no sign of danger pressed on, keen to make the jungle. There was a new spring in our step.

The jungle had become our paradise-in-waiting. I'd kept myself going by imagining cool pools into which I'd jump and swim and swim. Pin said the jungle was a place of mystery and wonder where magical things might happen. He said there were a great many stories of the jungle. "And not all of them end in tragedy," he declared.

For Jacques it promised sanctuary, a place where Tonton would be free to live. As we walked down the hill he began talking, more than I ever heard him talk. We could all stay in the jungle, he said, build a house from bamboo and vines, a tree house perhaps or find a cave. We could hunt for food and pick fruit from the trees and...

He went quiet mid-sentence. "What?" I said.

He shrugged. "I am a circus boy, born and raised in the circus, and circus boys and circus girls know all about creating make believe."

"Tell me about the circus – I wish I was a circus girl," I said and took his hand.

Perhaps it was the sight of the jungle and the relief that we were going to make it – Tonton was going to survive – that made Jacques talk and talk, as if his word tap was turned on.

The circus was all he'd known ever since he'd first opened his eyes as a baby, born in the soft straw of the tiger enclosure, his mother's hands held by his father on one side and Kamal the fire-eater on the other. It was his mother's idea because she loved the tigers as much as Jacques. Tonton's mother watched Jacques come into the world, tail swishing anxiously as Jacques' mother's screams were at last joined by that of her baby.

Jacques had the circus in his blood. He could somersault before he could walk (although his mother would tease him that it was nothing more than falling over while trying to walk).

He knew it was all an act, a pretend world; from the outside magical and fantastical and dazzling and sparkling. From the inside... well, all that glitters is not gold.

The circus is about dreaming, and dreams, at least in Jacques' experience, never come true.

"Oh Jacques," I said and squeezed his hand. He

seemed to feel for the first time we were holding hands and let go of mine.

His mother died soon after Vette arrived in the world. "The show must go on," said his father through a veil of tears. And it did. They travelled around Europe, Jacques' father scanning *Der Artist,* the newspaper for acrobats, and finding work here, there and everywhere. Once in Kharkov in Russia, the snow was over their knees outside the tent; yet the show, of course, began on time to a full house wrapped up in furs.

In time they came back to Paris and the Cirque Napoleon. Life was good: home was a couple of rooms in an apartment rather than a chilly caravan and walking to the circus down the Faubourg Saint Antoine, past the queues of carriages, pushing through the chattering crowds – everyone's excited when they come to the circus – the smell of fried potatoes and sweet meats. And performing, the thrill of the act.

It was here Jacques first went into the ring, drank in the ooohhhs and aaahhhs of the crowd, soaked up the applause. At first he would walk on a rolling ball, following Kamal as the fire-eater swallowed burning torches or set fire to his arms to gasps from the packed crowds. Then it was up to a low-level tightrope, sometimes with Merci the Monkey – they would hold hands and pretend they were about to fall off. Higher and higher he went until one unforgettable night he flew through the air high above the ring and was caught by the safe hands of his father.

He would never forget the smile on his father's upside down face – he was hanging from a swing – nor would he ever forget the look on his father's face several years later when he was taken away by two policemen. There had been an incident in a bar; some money had been stolen and of course it was the circus man who was suspected. There was a fight; again the circus man was blamed for injuring someone. He went to prison, far from Paris – a prison island from where few came home – because nobody trusts a circus man. Certainly not a judge, despite no evidence whatsoever. It was the citizen's word versus the circus man's word.

It left Jacques and Vette on their own. It was Kamal who came to their rescue. He was going to India, taking a travelling circus; there were fortunes to be made, reputations to be earned – the famous Lockhart brothers had gone to India as nobodies and returned as elephant trainers. Back in Europe they earned 70,000 francs a year, a fortune. And Kamal's circus needed acrobats. So Jacques and Vette came to India.

The crowds jostled in to see them. Kamal's eyes glinted as he counted each evening's take into his coffers, damp towels wrapped around his singed arms to cool them after the show. The morning rebellion reached Agra, he'd been cross with Jacques and Vette – they were running late. "Catch us up," he ordered and for some reason, despite being angry, hugged them both. It was as if he'd a sense of what was coming. He stared at The Top, shaking his head – there had been a delay in dismantling it; the labourers hadn't turned up. It too would be sent after them. Then he pulled himself into the driving seat of the leading cart and cracked the whip to signal the start of the circus's final journey.

Jacques shrugged in that way of his. Now it was just him, on his own, still a boy really even though he'd long since stopped thinking of himself as a child. He glanced round at me and Pin. I gave him my best motherly smile.

"You two are so alike," said Jacques. "Look at you!"

"How?" I said.

"Never!" said Pin.

"You walk the same, like a couple of baby giraffes on your long legs." He guffawed.

"But I have a shorter neck," declared Pin. I punched his arm and we all cackled with laughter – cackled because our throats were so dry – and between us Tonton padded along, tongue hanging out. I wondered if her spirits were soaring like ours. Could she sense we were approaching her future?

She didn't have much choice. Tonton would have to stay in the jungle whether we did or not. I knew what Jacques thought about it because he'd told me one afternoon while we were trying to rest, too hot to sleep.

"She has to live, even if it isn't with me, she has to live… I can't have another death on my hands. Not after Vette."

"It'll be all right," I promised him, crossing my fingers. I was doing a lot of that recently. "It will, you'll see."

The whooping and screeching of a family of monkeys woke me.

Tonton was sitting on the other side of the clearing, staring up into the tree occupied by the monkeys. Above her the langurs squatted in a row on a thick branch behaving very much as you'd expect monkeys to behave.

I pushed myself into a sitting position, leaning against the trunk of the broad tree we'd curled up beneath. I yawned and watched Tonton watching the langurs, trying to learn the ropes in her new home. She sat like a cat, her tail twitching back and forth.

I yawned again and rubbed my blurry eyes. Next to me Pin let out a quiet snore and mumbled something in his sleep. He talked a lot in his sleep, as if his mind

never
rested.
Next
to Pin,
Jacques lay
on his side, eyes
screwed shut,
either asleep
or wishing he was. His
legs were covered by a thin,
worn blanket with a large red splodge in the
middle.

It was already warm, warm and sticky; my clothes clung to me. I yawned once more. I felt clammy, my skin soaked in sweat.

I wish, I wish, I wish for a wash, clean clothes and somewhere dry and soft to sleep… for a whole day, no two days, no three, then breakfast brought to me in bed, mangoes and bananas and an orange, sliced up, and I'll eat as messily as I want. Then a plate of modak, made with sweet coconut. And after breakfast a swim in deep, cool water; wouldn't a swim be just wonderful, diving under, the water covering me...

A blanket? Why did Jacques have a blanket covering him in this heat? And where did he get it from? We hadn't brought blankets with us.

I shook my head; even my mind felt sticky. My head was leaning back against the tree and I rolled it to my left to look at the blanket again, another yawn rising within. The yawn was halfway out when I realised what the blanket and the red splodge were: a red splodge with legs, eight of them actually, and a body. My mouth remained open, the yawn dying away. I blinked and rubbed my eyes again just to be sure.

The large red spider was now sitting on the blanket, or to be precise the humungous red spider was now sitting in the middle of the web it had spun across Jacques' legs.

"J-J-J-J-Jacques, there's... there's..." I whispered. Pin muttered something in his sleep, Jacques lay still. My words drifted away, unheard by anyone. Apart, perhaps, from the spider. I was sure it was looking at me.

Across the clearing the langurs ceased their chatter,

instead taking on Tonton in a staring contest. The five monkeys stared down at the tiger; the tiger, tail still twitching, stared back at the monkeys. And, across the clearing, I stared at the spider and the spider stared at me.

Ever so slowly I picked up the large leaf I'd pulled off the tree the previous evening to use as a pretend bed cover – I like to have something over me when I sleep, it feels right. I narrowed my eyes, taking aim, then lifted the leaf over Pin and slid it on to Jacques. The spider retreated down Jacques' legs. I followed it with the leaf – I didn't want to harm the spider, no matter how scary it looked with its angry red body and hairy red legs. I just wanted to get it off Jacques. With a flick of my wrist I jerked the leaf, and fell sideways on to Pin, who in turn shot up, yelling in surprise.

"HUT JAO…"

Startled, Jacques too sat bolt upright, looked down at his legs and screamed. He scrambled to his feet, brushing at his legs.

"Enlève-moi ça, enlève-moi…" he cried. "Get it off me."

"Whoop, whoop, whoop," went the monkeys,

convinced this was some cunning plan devised by the tiger – the jungle's Queen of Cunning – to have them all for breakfast.

But the tiger's only concern was for Jacques. Tonton bounded across the clearing, eyes wide in alarm at Jacques' yells. So startled was she, she failed to stop and crashed into Jacques, sending them both tumbling to the ground.

"Tonton-non-non-non…"

Jacques' voice was muffled by having a tiger's chest covering his mouth. Tonton looked around as if she couldn't work out where her beloved Jacques had gone, then leapt to her feet when she found him beneath her. She stood over him and licked his face, making small grunting noises.

"What on earth was all that about?" said Pin, glaring at me.

"Spider… huge spider…"

My heart was pumping. I held my hands apart to demonstrate the size, my eyes searching the jungle floor.

"Where?" said Pin, lending his sharp eyes to the search.

"Gone," I said after one more good look around. My

attention switched to Tonton and Jacques. How on earth were we going to get the tiger to make a home for herself in the jungle, a home without Jacques? I looked at Pin and suspected he was thinking the exact same thing. Pin shook his head at me. I frowned a reply.

After a breakfast of a small handful of rasbharis each, we trekked deeper into the jungle; hot hours of warily and wearily pushing through thick vegetation. Pin led the way, slashing at the undergrowth with the machete and a large stick.

"To scare off any snakes, or spiders, or lizards, or scorpions," he explained; which was why we went warily, including Tonton, who stuck close to Jacques despite encouragements to go off and explore. Jacques tried throwing a stick into the undergrowth. The look Tonton gave him was clear: "I'm not a dog."

I found my own stick and clutched it tight, just in case. I didn't want any more spider alarms. I could feel sweat running down my back and arms, down my forehead. I kept having to stop to wipe my brow. Walking in the jungle drained you, like pulling the plug from a bath.

At last, sometime early in the afternoon, we came across a path – Pin made a guess at the time from the position of the sun and its angled rays through the holes in the canopy that gave the jungle its own roof.

The path was narrow, just wide enough to walk in single file, and little more than a line of beaten down grass.

"Deer track," said Pin and we followed him without a moment's hesitation.

Pin seemed to know where he was going. He was a certain boy, certain he was right. "I've read it," he'd state to settle any debate.

His knowledge was based on books he'd "borrowed" from the governor's library. He'd read one written by a British explorer that was supposed to tell you all about the jungle. Like most people in Agra, he'd never set foot in the jungle before. He knew where it was and how large it was because he'd studied the governor's maps. It was as if one look was enough to paint it in his mind.

I watched Pin as he marched off down the path with an energy I didn't feel. I think what he wanted more than anything else was to live a life worth putting in a book. He wanted adventure. Perhaps Jacques was right; me and Pin were the same.

"Sambar deer," Pin said about the track's creators, nodding his head. "The sambar deer hoots when alarmed. Its meat tastes much as well-hung venison from the highlands of Scotland..."

"What?" I looked at him. "The highlands of Scotland?"

"Um, that's what it said in the jungle book."

"We should follow it," suggested Jacques. "It must lead somewhere."

"Yes," said Pin. "Follow me." And we did.

Progress was quicker and easier on the deer track. Our spirits rose higher still when the path, having taking us through an even thicker part of the jungle where we had to duck beneath low-hanging leaves, vines and branches (after I'd given them a careful prod in case of spiders or snakes), led us into a clearing; the first we had seen since setting out that morning.

It was larger than the one we'd spent the night in, much larger.

"Oh my," I said, gazing around.

Pin had a pleased look on his face, and I'm not surprised. This was just as I'd imagined. On the far side of the clearing, a steep rocky hill climbed quickly and down it splashed a waterfall, gathering at its foot into a large pool. The track led straight to the pool. There were hoof prints in the slope that slipped into the water and other animal prints too.

"Come on," I said and ran across the clearing. "I'm going in."

"Wait!"

"No!"

Pin and Jacques matched each other in their alarm. I glanced back.

"Scaredy-cats," I yelled.

I scrambled up the rocks that curved around the top end of the pool. At the top, I unwrapped my sari, dropped it to the ground and decided that was quite enough undressing and leapt.

"Long live us!" I yelled causing a bird somewhere nearby to squawk an alarm call and then I hit the water.

Once upon a time I found jumping in hard, standing for an age on the diving rock above Loch Laddich before clambering down and wading in from the bank. "Next time," was all Grannie said. Next time, next time, next time and then… I did it. Straight in and as soon as I'd done it once that was it: shutting my eyes as I jump, then opening them again under water, cheeks puffed full of air, kicking for the surface and the sense of freedom; there's nothing to hold you back.

I kicked down, deep as I could go and ran my hands across the stones on the bottom. The water was murky, not as murky as the loch and not as cold. In fact, it wasn't cold at all – more like a bath just after the "turn", when the heat has gone but there is still warmth there.

I let myself rise slowly towards the surface, the water clearing enough for me to be able to make out the blurred figures of Pin, Jacques and Tonton, two scaredy-cats and one very big cat, on the bank, scanning the surface.

"Beeeaaaa!" A muffled call drifted through the water.

My head broke the surface, but only reluctantly. I wish I could hold my breath for longer. I practise every time I have a bath and I'm getting better.

"Bea!"

I snatched a breath and dived again. I love it when the water closes over you. I pulled hard and dived down, this time towards the waterfall. Here the pool was deeper than I'd expected and the deeper you went, the cooler the water. I let myself glide upwards again, pulled back to the real world by my lungs demanding air and surfaced again, this time in the middle of the pool. I trod water.

"Come on in – it's beautiful. I feel new."

The boys stood on the edge, hands on hips; neither prepared to take another step. Tonton paced up and down the bank. There was no way she was going in either.

"Pah," I said and blew a mouthful of water in their direction. "Boys!"

"There could be snakes in there," said Pin.

"So?

I arched my body and dived down once more. This time I came out as close to the boys as I could, spraying them with water, kicking at them from the shallows. Tonton leapt away, looking more cat-like than ever. I ran round to the rocks, spread out my sari and sat down on it, waiting for the sun to dry me. My remaining clothes clung to me, wet and cooling. I felt 100 times better. A parrot, bright green, darted across the clearing. I followed its flight, open-mouthed.

"This should be our camp, shouldn't it?" I said as the boys clambered up to join me. "We can make a shelter here in the rocks, get away from all those spiders and creepy crawlies – those big leaves can make a roof, we can put sticks across then cover it with leaves and vines. We can build a fire for night time, that'll scare away the snakes. We can make a bow and arrow and hunt; there's lots to eat in the jungle."

I beamed at them – one of those smiles that grows and grows because your chest feels like it's swelling with happiness. "This can be our home… can't it? Yes, that's it, we'll wait here until the fighting stops then we can go and find George. I'm sure he'd love to have two big brothers. We could take Tonton as well, she could live in the garden then we wouldn't need a night watchman…"

I paused because Jacques and Pin were both shaking their heads.

"What?"

Now they both looked away.

"You're a couple of proper miseries – go on, get in the water, it'll make you feel better. A swim always makes you feel better about life."

"I don't like water," muttered Jacques.

"I cannot swim," said Pin. "I have never been in the water beyond my knees. I've watched people do it in the Jumna. It does not look that difficult."

"I'll teach you," I said, leaping up, not wanting to allow them to dampen my mood. "I'll teach you to swim and you can teach me about India, tell me more of your stories. I want to learn."

"Yes, that is fair," said Pin, leaping up too.

First we decided to build our shelter.

"We must not be caught out by darkness in the jungle," said Pin.

"No," I said, "we mustn't."

Pin and me took the machete and went to cut some bamboo while Jacques gathered the largest leaves he could find, lifting them carefully in case a sleeping snake or spider were resting underneath.

"We can survive in the jungle," I said. "I've read stories about people being shipwrecked and living a wonderful life in the jungle… and they didn't have a tiger on their side."

"We shall see," said Pin. "Cut here."

I swung the machete.

"Harder," instructed Pin, "bamboo is strong."

After I'd finished cutting – which made me sweaty again – Pin hunted around the jungle floor.

"Aha!" he said and pulled hard at what looked like a spear beginning to rise out of the ground. "Bamboo shoot."

It didn't take him long to gather an armful and on the way back to the waterfall he explained how we could peel and boil the shoots.

"There is all the food we need, right here in the jungle. If we can find a tamarind tree, bananas perhaps, mangoes… then we shall have even more choice. We can live like kings."

He looked pleased with himself.

"How are we going to cook these shoots?"

Pin looked less pleased with himself. He thought for a while. "I'll think of something."

While Jacques and I finished off the shelter, watched by Tonton sunning herself on a rock above us like a newly crowned Queen of the Jungle, Pin disappeared.

He returned an hour or so later, this time looking hot and bothered. He ducked into the shade of the shelter and slumped down against the rock face that made up the far wall.

"Pingali!" I exclaimed. Grannie used to use my full name when she was particularly pleased with me… or when she was cross. I was looking at what Pin had in his hand – a pan. Pin's pan. I giggled. He pulled two triangular pieces of stone out of the pan.

"Two stones?" I was less impressed.

"Flints," said Pin, "for lighting fires; you gather dry grass and twigs and use the flint to get a spark." He made an imaginary fire with his hands and then blew gently on it. "You blow on it and the ember becomes a flame." He raised his hands. "Puuufff."

I clapped my hands together. "I think you are the cleverest person I've ever met, Pingali Rao. Isn't he Jacques?"

Jacques nodded. Now we really could make a life in the jungle.

"What's the matter?" Jacques could see something wasn't right with Pin.

"Perhaps it's nothing," said Pin. "Come on let's pick some grass, we can leave it out on the rocks to dry in the sun so it's ready to catch fire. We must gather sticks too, for the fire."

It was later, after a dinner of bamboo shoots and mango. We were sitting around the fire, which had lit on the second go. The bamboo was surprisingly tasty if quite chewy. All prepared by Pin. He should have been beaming, as pleased with himself as a magician who had just pulled a white rabbit from his hat for the first time.

But the flickering flames lit up a worried face. Pin stared into the fire.

"What is it, Pin?"

He looked through the flames at me.

I was cross with Pin, despite everything he'd done. His gloomy mood was pulling me down, and Jacques. It hung over the fire like a grey cloud. Why can't he be happy with what we've done?

"The pot, the flints," he said. "I found them…"

"I know, brilliant you."

"It looked like they'd been hidden…"

"Hidden?"

"Yes, which means someone hid it…"

"So?"

"You don't hide something unless you want to keep it, to use it… use it again…"

"Someone will come back for it – that's what you're saying?" Jacques leaned forward. "Someone has made a camp here before us, someone who will be back here looking for their pot and flints."

"Exactly," said Pin. "But who?"

That first night in our new camp none of us slept much. Our tension was picked up by Tonton. She paced around, offering glimpses of her stripes as she strode back and forth by the fire.

In the end we all dozed off, even Jacques who was supposed to be keeping watch. And in the morning all was fine. For a couple of days we kept a wary eye out and ear cocked but nobody came, and, as the days passed, our worries dwindled.

I even got Pin into the pool. He splashed and yelled and managed a few strokes; our laughter joined together and rose into the blue sky. Jacques sat on the bank and shook his head. There was no way he was getting in.

Pin learnt quickly. One afternoon he managed to

swim like a dog across to the other side with me. We scrambled out and waved at Jacques.

"Look!" I said. Tonton stepped into the water and waded towards us. Soon only her head was visible. "I didn't know tigers could swim."

"Oh, yes," said Pin, "they are very good in the water. I read it in..."

"One of the governor's books." I finished his sentence for him.

Tonton reached our side and padded up to us. She rubbed her head against my leg and I tickled behind the tiger's ear. I did it without thinking, like it was the most natural thing in the world to have a tiger as a friend.

Tonton studied the jungle. She swished her tail. I turned to see if Jacques would follow his tiger across, and when I looked back it was to see Tonton disappearing into the trees.

"Tonton," I said.

Pin put a hand on my arm. "Leave her," he said. "This is what she must do."

I watched until she was out of sight. It didn't take long – a tiger, with its camouflage stripes, is hard to spot in the jungle. There was one last shimmer of black and golden brown and then the stillness returned. Somewhere deeper in the jungle a monkey screeched.

"Come on," I said, trying to ignore the beginnings of a sinking feeling. "Race you to Jacques."

Tonton came back a few hours later as darkness was falling and sat down on the rock above the shelter with what sounded like a tired but satisfied sigh. We'd just finished our meal – bamboo shoots as always – and were discussing whether we dared catch and cook any of the large insects that strolled through the camp day and night. The biggest fright we'd had was when I woke one night with one of them taking a short cut across my face. I sat up and screamed – who wouldn't have? It was huge. Jacques suggested we could make a spear and hunt something.

"What?"

"Snakes?"

"Urgh."

"Arjuna, the greatest of the Pandavas, he once shot five arrows into the eye of a fish with one shot. He was a great hunter, the greatest."

"Well, he's not here to help us is he…"

"A spear is easier to make than a bow and arrow." Jacques interrupted me. He could sense my mood. Sometimes when I feel myself falling, getting dragged down, I get cross with people – I can't stop myself and then I feel even worse afterwards.

"I don't think I could eat another bamboo shoot ever ever," I declared, trying to stop myself falling. I added a couple more "evers" just to make certain I couldn't be misunderstood by the boys. Even a slice of snake might be better than another bamboo shoot.

"I read of the mahua tree which has flowers you can eat but you must look out for sloth bears because they..." began Pin.

"Shhh," said Jacques, cocking his head to one side. "Did you hear that?"

"What?"

"Shhh."

"Don't ask me a question then shush me... oh, did you hear that?" I stood up.

"Sounded like a call," said Jacques.

A loose stone rattled down the rocks, kicked by a misplaced footstep. It was already dark. When darkness came in the jungle, it came like a blown-out candle.

"An animal?" wondered Pin. His breathing was getting faster. So was my heart... it was beating so quickly it felt as if it was thumping against my rib cage.

The boys stood up next to me, backs to the fire. We narrowed our eyes and squinted into the darkness. What was out there? I took Pin's hand and squeezed it. He squeezed back. "Don't leave me," my squeeze meant.

Tonton stood with us. Her tail was high: her alert signal. Something was coming towards us from the jungle.

"We should put the fire out," whispered Pin.

"Too late," said Jacques.

Tonton grunted and slid away into the darkness.

"Keep watch," said Pin and let go of my hand.

"Where are you going?"

"The machete – it's in the shelter, I'll..."

"Wait," said Jacques, "I've got it."

He raised the machete. It flashed in the light of the fire.

"Tonton... Tonton... ou est tu?" Jacques' words whispered out into the night.

The fire crackled and spat and we all jumped.

Pin grinned. Me and Jacques grinned back. That's what can happen when you're really scared. When a fright turns out to be nothing, the next reaction is to laugh. It's relief. So you smile when you least expect it.

A moment later and three grins were frozen on our faces and my busy heart leapt into my mouth where it did several somersaults before plunging back to its proper position. A man stepped into the light, as if he'd been hiding behind a dark curtain, had drawn it aside and stepped into the room.

He wore a dirty red coat missing one sleeve. His trousers might once have been parade-ground white but were now on a scale between very dark brown and black. On his head was a British officer's sun helmet but he had no badges or signs of an officer's rank on his coat.

His beard, thick, dark and dirty, hung down to his chest, across which were criss-crossed bandoliers in a thick and threatening X. Two pistols were shoved into the bandoliers. I could see both were cocked and loaded, ready to fire (that time with Private Coombe learning to load pistols had not been wasted).

As was the pistol he held in his right hand. In his left he brandished a fearsome tulwar, its long, curved blade making our machete look no scarier than a butter knife: a man ready for a fight.

"What's all this then – a vicar's bloomin' tea party?" His voice was a snarl.

Pin and Jacques took a step back towards the fire. So did I.

"Drop it," ordered the Englishman, for that's where his voice placed him. He gestured at the machete with his pistol.

Jacques shook his head.

"We're on the same side," I suggested, as brightly as I could. "We're lost you see, trying to get to the hill station at Hulla… can you help us?"

Hulla was where George lived with Aunt Celia. It was the first place that came to mind. I had no idea where it was, but it occurred to me as it was where I would like to be at that exact moment.

"I'm not on nobody's side," growled the man. "Now drop it."

"Deserter," volunteered Pin.

"What's it gotta do with you, you scrawny native wretch?"

"Nothing, kind sir, pray excuse my…"

"Shut up." The man pointed the pistol at Pin. "Or I'll shut you up good and proper."

He swung his attention to Jacques. "Now, drop it or I'll shoot you."

"I'd do what he says."

We swung round to see another man step into the light. He too wore a mishmash of scruffy British army clothes. He had a smudge of stubble around his cheeks and chin which made him look as dirty as his uniform.

"Now," he added and raised his own pistol to point straight at me. "Or the girl gets it."

There was a moment of silence, the hiss of the fire the only sound. I swallowed and opened my mouth. Then it happened.

When a tiger attacks, it does so without a sound. They say in India the first you know is when you feel its hot breath on the back of your neck. The second man didn't even have time to turn. Tonton leapt into the light and smashed into him, sending him crashing to the ground.

"Bloody 'ell," said the first deserter – for that is what they were, desperate runaways from the army, robbing and murdering their way across India. He stepped towards Tonton, pointing his pistol, seeking a clean shot as his companion tried to beat off the tiger.

I seized my chance and made a leap of my own – leaping without thinking as usual – but there was nothing silent about my attack.

"Rarrrrggghhh!" I roared and flung myself at the first man.

He spun round towards this equally unexpected attack but couldn't bring his pistol to bear before I was on him. I hit him head first in the stomach, a copper-topped human battering ram.

"Offffffftt," he said and dropped his sword, but kept a finger hooked through the trigger guard of his pistol.

I ran my hands across him, feeling for one of the other pistols. He straightened up and tried to push me away, gasping for breath. He smelt terrible. Him, his clothes, their rotten scent filled my nostrils. I felt the smooth wood of a pistol butt, hooked my fingers around it and yanked as hard as I could. He clamped a hand down and there was an almighty roar from the pistol. The press of our bodies muffled the sound but still it seemed as if someone had screamed fury into my ears. Together we fell to the ground.

"Bea!" yelled Pin and seized hold of the man's nearest arm to try to pull him off me. Jacques grabbed the machete and went to help Tonton. Not that the tiger needed his help.

The man I'd attacked was yelling, in pain and anger. The bullet from his pistol had grazed his foot, and he had Pin and me sitting on him trying to get hold of his third pistol. He swung a fist and knocked Pin off, freeing himself to pull the pistol from his bandolier. He put his free hand on my head and pushed me away. Some of my hair caught in one of his rings.

"Owwww!" I screeched, swinging my hands like an exploding Catherine wheel. Rage pulsed through me.

He sat up, trying to give himself room to fire.

He aimed the pistol at me. I looked right down the barrel.

"Tonton!" I yelled.

His finger curled around the trigger, but before

he could pull it there was a blur of movement to his right. He swung the pistol round and pulled the trigger at the same moment Tonton launched her second attack.

Tonton was already into her leap when the pistol roared right into my ears. The sound of our desperate battle was snatched from me. I watched what unfolded with ears ringing.

Tonton thudded into the man, pinning him to the ground, his head thumping against a rock as he was pushed backwards. He was knocked clean out. Tonton lay on top of him. Neither man nor tiger moved.

Time stopped. It felt an age before anyone said or did anything.

To this day I have never talked with the others about what happened that terrible night – it has become an unspoken rule that we never, ever mention it – so I have no idea how long we froze before I clambered unsteadily to my feet.

"Tonton?"

My voice sounded distant, echoing in my own head. I rubbed my ears. One of them made a popping sound. I looked down on the still tiger, the man's legs and arms sticking out at odd angles beneath her.

"Tonton?" I saw Pin mouth. He too had got to his feet. Blood was trickling from his nose where the man's punch had caught him.

"Non… non…" said Jacques. "Non, Tonton… non."

His voice sounded strange, distant, not real. He crumpled to the ground alongside his tiger, tried to pull her over. He wanted her to roll over and lift a paw so he could scratch her stomach. He wanted her off the man. He had to get her off this man: the man who'd taken her life.

"Non," said Jacques once more. He put his arms around Tonton's neck, pressed his face into her fur and, as my other ear popped and my hearing came back in full, Jacques started to cry.

It took most of the night to bury Tonton. It was Pin who dragged us up and made us get on with it. The ground was hard so all we could do was claw a shallow dent into which we laid the tiger. We stacked rocks on top of her until she was covered and kept piling them on, determined to stop jackals from getting at her. Jacques cried a lot as we worked. I cried as well and I think Pin did too, but after a while the tears dried up. They do. The show must, well, you know…

When we were done we stood next to the grave. Jacques sniffed, swallowed hard.

"Au revoir, Tonton," he said.

"She saved us… saved our lives and lost hers," I said and tightened my grip on Jacques' hand. Pin stood on the other side of him, his left hand holding Jacques' right so we were all connected.

We stood in silence for a while, until a groan came from behind us. Jacques spun round and pulled one of the pistols from his waistband.

The first man, the one who'd shot Tonton, sat up and held his head in his hands.

Jacques walked towards him and raised the pistol. The man looked up, and flinched.

"No," he moaned, "don't… don't kill me."

He snivelled and put his head back in his hands, as if they would protect him from a bullet.

"Jacques," said Pin, and stepped after him. I put out a hand and pulled Pin back.

Jacques stood over the man, pointing the pistol at him.

"Alleeeez," he hissed. "Go, take your friend… I will count to ten and then I will shoot at you both."

The man risked a glance up at Jacques.

"ALLEZ!"

The deserter staggered to his feet and limped to his companion. Jacques followed him with the pistol. I knew he wanted to pull the trigger, wanted revenge for Tonton.

And revenge for Vette I suspected – for everything that had happened to him since he came to India and probably long before that. I watched his finger curl around the trigger. I held my breath. His finger straightened and I breathed again.

"ALLEZ!" Jacques yelled again. The man hauled his limp friend to his feet – I didn't know whether he was dead or alive – and began dragging him towards the jungle. He looked back over his shoulder, his face twisted.

"This is dark magic… dark magic, evil. If I see any of you again… I'll kill you… I'll burn you alive…"

"Un… deux…" began Jacques. He let his pistol arm drop as the men disappeared into the pre-dawn gloom. I put my arms around him; the pistol fell to the ground. Pin linked his long arms around us both.

After a while, Jacques shrugged us off.

"Now, we go on," he said.

Pin nodded. "Yes, we can't stay here – they'll come back, maybe more of them. It's not safe."

"So where?" said Jacques.

I knew what I had to do. "Find Hulla, find George." I nodded at my own suggestion. "I must find my brother, get him away from all of this… this horror, make him safe. I'm his big sister."

"Then where?" Jacques looked into the distance. The hoot of a bird filled the silence. I think it was a parrot.

"We'll find somewhere," I said. I don't know how I sounded to Pin and Jacques but it didn't sound very convincing to me.

"I could take you back to Agra, after we find your brother?" suggested Pin.

"What about you?"

Pin shrugged – just like Jacques, as if he'd been taking lessons. "I can't go back there – they'll kill me, hang me, they'll think I'm a spy."

"No," I said, the conviction back in my voice. "We're not going anywhere without you."

"I'm Indian – you two, you are Europeans… wherever we go people will stop us being together."

"Not in the circus," said Jacques, his voice suddenly angry. "In the circus everyone is equal. That's what Kamal says."

"Well, that's settled, let's run away and join the circus," I said. I tried to make my voice light, tried to lift us out of the dark. "Shall we?"

Pin nodded as well. "I should like that," he said and we both looked expectantly at Jacques as if he could make it happen just like that. He shook his head.

"You're crazy, you two."

"Yes, but just imagine..." I began.

I was still telling them my imaginings – it helped keep the thought of what had happened to Tonton at bay – when we set off at first light. We hadn't wanted to risk the jungle in the dark with the two deserters somewhere out there. We took a pistol each, unloaded, as I insisted it wasn't safe to travel with them charged. We took the machete and left their sword. We also took a beaten-up army pack I removed from the first man when he was unconscious; in it were the bullets and charges for the pistols but more importantly a water bottle and some chapattis, raisins and potatoes.

Pin led the way. I told him the name of the hill station – Hulla – where George lived and the district. Pin tutted and sighed and hummed and hahhed. He drew a map in the dust with a stick and explained how we should get there. It meant going back past Agra and then turning south-westwards for several days – Pin was not sure precisely where the station was but would ask directions when we got closer.

"I will never go back to Agra..." butted in Jacques, his voice catching that note of anger again. It made him sound more French. "Never – it's because of them we are 'ere and Vette is dead and Tonton is dead. We must... all three of us – we must stay together."

He nodded at us. "Listen to me... there is a book, my favourite book, given to me by my papa our last Christmas together. *Les Trois Mousquetaires*..."

"Three blind mice?"

"Non." Jacques looked annoyed with my suggestion. "Just listen, Bea... Mousquetaires, they're fighters, great fighters for the king, and they save the queen."

"I've not read this book..." began Pin.

"Shhhh," hissed Jacques. "Listen, both of you... It's what they say in the book..." He pulled out his pistol and pointed to the sky. "The musketeers, they say 'All for one and one for all.' They are inseparable. That shall be us, you see? Now say it..."

I lifted my pistol, Pin made it three. "Now," said Jacques, "with me..."

And we said it together.

"All for one and one for all."

As we followed the path back through the jungle, Pin insisted Jacques tell us the story of *Les Trois*

Mousquetaires. Jacques begun hesitantly; he wasn't used to storytelling. But it didn't take long for him to find his voice because who doesn't like telling stories?

There was the occasional hiccup when he couldn't think of the right English word and we tried to help him. Otherwise the tales of the musketeers getting out of sticky situations just in time to save the day kept us going to the very edge of the jungle.

"So you see," said Jacques as we left the jungle and headed for the road back to Agra, "why I say we need to stay together because three is better than two or one."

It lifted our spirits and they needed lifting. All for one and one for all. The journey from Agra had been scary and exhausting and the thought of retracing our footsteps – without our Tonton, who'd become part of us – filled me with dread.

We decided to walk through the first day and were lucky. We saw no one. We went on into the night and when dawn glimmered on the horizon found an abandoned house hidden from the road by some trees. We collapsed together in a corner, our spirits tumbling with us, covered by what remained of the roof. It would keep the sun off while we slept.

We munched a handful of raisins, swallowed some water then lay down and stared up at a half moon shuffling wearily across the sky as day approached.

"Once," began Pin. He always thought a story would help. So did I usually. "Ganesha gathered a great collection of sweets, his favourite laddoos – Motichoor laddoos I would have thought – and was carrying them back to his home on Mount Kailash. But he had too many so could not see where he was going and the great Ganesha tripped. His sweets went everywhere as he fell. And looking down on it all, the moon laughed at Ganesha, laughed at his trip and his sweets being scattered across the land and Ganesha got angry – because everyone gets angry sometimes – and he shouted at the moon and told the moon that no longer would he be full every night. And that is why there is only half a moon up there now... Ganesha... oh, Ganesha help us..."

His voice trailed off.

"I don't think Ganesha is with us." I spoke in little more than a whisper. "I don't think anyone is with us, Pin."

Pin sat up. "He is... I know he is – you'll see. He'll never abandon us."

"Ouch," I said and opened my eyes.

A man was standing over me, holding a sword with which he'd prodded me awake.

I blinked and rubbed my side.

"Up," said the man and gestured with his sword.

I pushed myself to my feet with the help of the wall. The man prodded Pin and then Jacques, who was lying on his side facing the wall. Jacques rolled around and tried to get himself up. The man placed a foot on his back and shoved him down.

"One at a time," he ordered. He pointed at me. "Search her."

Two other men came forward. There were a large group of them packed into the shell of the ruined house, all wearing a version of the same outfit: baggy white trousers and baggy white shirts tied around their middles with a swish of red cloth, from which protruded an array of daggers and swords.

Their faces matched their weapons, angry and sharp. Rough hands pulled me away from the others. One wrenched the pistol from me. A finger pointed in my face.

"Spy – you're a spy."

"Death to spies," someone at the other end of the room shouted. More voices joined in.

I opened my mouth but no words came out.

"Yes, death to spies."

"All British spies must die."

"Kill them."

"Leave her alone – she's no spy."

Pin's voice carried over the others. He was pulled to his feet and pushed against the wall; his pistol fell out of his waistband and clunked on to the floor.

The man who'd prodded us awake – he wore a white turban and had a gold necklace hanging around his neck – pressed his tulwar against Pin's throat.

Pin gulped and pressed himself as hard as he could against the wall.

"I wouldn't waste your breath on her – not when you have your own case to make. What's an Indian boy doing helping these goralogs? For your sake I hope they took you prisoner because the punishment for helping the British is death."

"All for one and one for all," said Pin.

"What?" said the leader.

"Give him to us, we'll kill the traitor."

"Death to the traitor, death to the traitor."

"WAIT!"

The leader looked down at Jacques. He kept his sword pressed to Pin's throat. Jacques stood up slowly and put his hands out, palms down, a suggestion everyone stay calm.

"Let me explain – we're not British. Nous sommes français... we are French, from the circus at Agra – acrobats, we're acrobats..."

"What's an acrobat?"

"The flying men..."

"Men who can fly?"

"Has he got wings?"

"Does he have a carpet?"

"Man can't fly."

"He must be a spirit – quick hold him tight."

"Kill him… before he flies away."

"SILENCE!"

The leader removed his sword from Pin's throat to wave it in the air to reinforce his order.

"Bring them – we'll take them to the rani and the great rani will decide their fate."

"Prostrate yourselves before her Highness, the rani of Jhansi, our Queen feared by all Englishmen."

A shove in Jacques' back emphasised the point as we stumbled across the village square. "On your knees, dogs."

"NO!"

Jacques and Pin kept their heads bowed. Only I looked up. A small woman, slight in stature, grown-up but no taller than me, dropped from a magnificent chestnut horse. At first glance she appeared dressed as a man, a turban of the whitest white on her head and the same baggy white shirt and white trousers as her soldiers. But there were differences: she wore a broad golden belt from which dangled a golden dagger with a diamond glittering on the end of its handle. A pearl necklace was wrapped around her throat and gold bracelets and anklets jingled as she stepped towards us on bare feet. Her long dark hair was tied into a plait.

"No human being is a dog; a man is a man and a woman is a woman and I receive all equally."

Her voice was smooth as honey, yet strong, certain. It sounded bigger than her. Yet it was not the most remarkable thing about her. That was her eyes. The rani of Jhansi had eyes like precious gems; eyes that won women and men to her side and made them follow her into battle. They persuaded people to live and die for her.

"Rise and approach me to plead your case."

We shuffled forward on our knees, not ready to risk standing in her presence. Two more women slid from white horses and stood either side of her, her maids of honour, dressed like their queen but without the golden belt. Instead of daggers they had tulwas in their plain belts. When the rani went into battle her maids of honour rode either side of her, ready to sacrifice themselves to protect their queen.

I took a deep breath, stood up, stepped in front of the boys and executed my best curtsey – maybe all those boring hours in Miss Goodenough's class had some worth after all.

"Your Majesty," I began, "this is the Great Romanini."

I had found my voice again, and had the glimmer of an idea. Thanks to Jacques. I gestured at Jacques, who bowed so low his fringe nearly brushed the ground.

"The Great Romanini is the greatest acrobat the world has seen – he flies through the air with the greatest of ease, he'll have you gasping in amazement..."

"Who are you?" interrupted the rani, although I suppose queens are allowed to interrupt.

"I, um..." I glanced at Jacques. Here goes... "... I am Juliette, and I perform up there..." I gestured to the sky "... hand-in-hand with the Great Romanini..."

Jacques flung a glance at me. I ignored it.

"And who is he? Can he fly as well?" A soft smile played across the rani's face.

Pin repeated Jacques' bow and outdid him for bendiness – his forehead introduced itself to the ground.

"Your most gracious Majesty, I am trying only to help the Great Romanini and, er, Juliette find a way to escape the terrible troubles that have gripped our land. They are innocents in a struggle that has nothing to do with them."

The rani studied him, then turned her gaze to Jacques and me in turn. I could feel the rani's eyes digging deep within me.

"The sensible decision is to have you executed; you are probably spies and I cannot afford to take risks."

"But, your Maj…" I began.

"SILENCE!" The rani gestured at me. "We are in the midst of a life or death struggle. If I am weak, I will die and my people will be enslaved again."

I gripped my hands in front of me to stop them shaking.

"Come on then," said the turbaned man who'd brought us to see the rani. "The great rani has made her decision."

I looked up and locked eyes with the rani. I angled my chin up and out.

"Wait…" The rani raised a hand. "Great acrobats you say. I heard talk of the circus that came to Agra and I have seen with my own eyes the circus tent which is still there on the plain before the city."

She kept her eyes on me.

"I am not a cruel ruler, I am fair. So I will give you a chance… prove to me you are who you say you are – prove to me you are the acrobats of Agra and you will live."

The sun was setting as we approached Agra, the great fort floating above it in the soft glow of the dying day. A column of pitch-black smoke rose in a straight line from within the city. A fleet of lights twinkled on the Jumna; the remaining residents in the city floated lamps down the sluggish river and prayed for an end to the terrors all around.

"Roll up, roll up," I whispered, catching sight of the circus Top. It was flooded with the sun's daily farewell. In India the sun likes to bow out with a royal reminder to everyone it will be back again tomorrow, come what may.

We were riding on an elephant, the three of us and a guard. I'd always wanted to see an elephant. But not like this. We'd bumped into the rani and a section of her army on a scouting mission – the rani always led from the front. They knew the British were coming but not when or how many or where from, and the rani wanted to know so she and her army would be ready for the great battle that would have to be fought.

We weren't actually on the elephant's back – only the mahout, the elephant's guide, sat directly on it. Passengers were left to hang on as we rocked around a wooden platform tied to the elephant's large and wobbly back.

There were three elephants in the convoy. Scouts on the first one and the rani's bodyguards crammed on the third. Behind the elephants came a cluster of horsemen, bristling with

swords and pistols led by the rani and her maids of honour, the rani astride her distinctive chestnut mare. She rode easily, a natural horsewoman, reins in one hand, the other resting on her hip.

With nightfall fast approaching, the British patrols, sent to scavenge for food, were safely locked up in the fort. It meant that everything outside the elephant-thick, red walls was the rani's for the night, including the Big Top.

The flag crowning the tent fluttered in the evening breeze. As we approached we began to see the Top had not escaped undamaged. On one side the canvas had been burnt off – somehow the fire had gone out before it engulfed the entire Top – and the wooden stands inside had been smashed to pieces, much of the wreckage taken away to use as firewood.

We lurched forward as the elephant bent its front knees and sat down.

"Can you do this Bea?" said Pin as we waited to get out. His eyes darted here and there, betraying his anxiety. Which was fair enough – as was the question. If I couldn't, then… well, that didn't bear thinking about.

"She can do it," said Jacques and swung a leg over the platform. He dropped to the ground and held a hand up. "Come on."

We walked into the Top, nobody paying us much attention – the guards were fussing around the rani, finding a place for her to sit for our trial by tightrope. Others kept watch towards Agra.

Flaming torches were carried into the Top and lashed into place. They cast a flickering light towards its roof. I glanced up and swallowed. Could I?

"It's just like we practised in the fort," said Jacques. He bent forward and touched the palms of his hands on the ground. "Come, we must get ready, get yourself loosened up – you can't fly if you're tense."

"It's high," said Pin.

Jacques glared at him. I swallowed again. My legs were made of lead.

Jacques pulled me towards him, gripping my arms tight. "Listen," he said. "I could tell you the net will catch you if you fall, but if you fall we all fall. So this is what we are going to do."

He leaned forward and whispered into my ear. I nodded, once, twice.

A guard came over, his eyes shining bright.

"See," said Jacques, "nobody can ever go to the circus and not be excited. The show…"

"Must go on," I whispered. My mouth felt dry. I looked at Jacques, then at Pin. "I won't let you down – I promise, Pingali."

"And I won't let you fall," replied Jacques and smiled at me, the broadest smile I'd ever seen from him. This must be what he had looked like to Vette each night before they took to the heavens. This is what I've wanted to do from that evening I sat open-mouthed between Aunt Constance and Primrose in this very place and fell head over heels for the Great Romanini.

"Get on with it," ordered the guard. "The rani is waiting."

"Very well," said Jacques. He took my hand and bowed towards the rani. I copied him.

Jacques let go of my hand and nodded at me. "It's time," he said. "Allez huuup."

"Just like in the courtyard?"

"Just like in the courtyard."

"Allez huuup." I echoed Jacques and sprang on to my hands.

While I upside-down walked, Jacques whirled

into a somersault to make his starting position. He was ready to give the performance of his young life (which he needed to if he wanted it to become an old life). He grabbed the rope and pulled himself quickly upwards.

What he'd said to me was that if he could dazzle rani and her guards, he could divert their attention from me. If he could convince their eyes, their minds would follow. And if… if I could do one part, just one part, of dear Vette's act, this would work.

To do just one part would mean I had to concentrate harder than I'd ever concentrated before. On the far side of the ring from Jacques, I flipped back on to my feet and leapt up the same rope Vette had scaled that happy night. It felt a lifetime ago; it was a lifetime ago, a different lifetime, a different me. I pulled myself up and up, following in Vette's handprints, my arms beginning to ache. There was a gasp from the rani's men down below and I glanced across the ring. Jacques was into his act, swinging from the bar.

I was nearly at my bar. "Don't look down, don't look down," I whispered as I reached up for it.

My hand stretched and caught hold of it. But I'd moved too quickly and the bar swung, taking me with it, hanging on by one hand. Our lives were hanging by my left hand.

A shout reached me from below – a cry of alarm from Pin. I shook my head. Forget about Pin, forget about Jacques, forget about the rani. Think only about me.

As the bar swung back, I swung my other hand up, not quickly or hard, just in the rhythm of the swing. I caught the bar and swung a couple more times. I had to get the timing spot on to make the small platform the tightrope was secured to. It was just big enough for a pair of feet.

"Allez huuuppp," I said, louder this time, confidence beginning to filter through my veins. I *can* do this. I let go of the bar, followed my legs on to the platform, grasped at the pole that rose to the roof to hold up the platform and tightrope, and clung on. I was breathing hard, but I'd done it… the easy part (easy compared to what was to come).

Jacques, after performing a couple of twirls and swirls to keep all eyes on him, was in position on his platform at the far end of the tightrope. He threw an encouraging smile my way, and I tossed one back. I closed my eyes and imagined, like I did in my bedroom when I was all on my own. Imagined packed stands below, girls and boys craning their necks to stare into the circus heavens and wishing they could be like me, like the girl on the posters, the girl whose name the ringmaster had proclaimed to one and all, the girl who flew through the air without a care in the world.

I reached down and unhooked the balancing pole that hung beneath the platform, where Vette had returned it after her final act. It was lighter than I expected, so light it felt as if it floated in the air.

I swung my left foot out and placed it on the tightrope, feeling the rope's roughness on my bare feet. I took the deepest breath of my life, found a spot to fix my eyes on, raised my right foot… this was it, no going back now… and swung that in front of my left.

Off I went. The left, now the right, the pole held in my hands, swaying ever so slightly, left, right, left, right, two more and I'd be in the middle. The middle; I let my front leg slide away, sent my back one in the opposite direction. And there it was, I was doing the splits, just as I had time after time on Grannie's front lawn. Except this time I was balanced on a tightrope, goodness knows how many feet above… STOP. I hurried the thought from my head and dropped my legs down so I was straddling the tightrope (it was too risky for me to try and stay doing the splits while Jacques leapt over me).

Jacques stepped out from his end. It was like he danced along the tightrope. He approached rapidly; I could feel the tightrope swaying, straining at the knots that kept it in place.

For a split second I thought he was going to walk right into me; instead he yelled "Allezzz huuppp!" and somersaulted over me. I couldn't see him land and for a moment I thought he'd missed, such was the lack of impact on the rope.

A loud cheer rose from below. Pin could see our way out. But up in the top of the Top there was still work for us to do. I let go of the pole and it dropped to the net far below. I couldn't regain my feet on the tightrope while holding the pole – one day I would be as good as Vette, but not yet.

An idea sprang into my head. Why not? I'd done it on the wobbly branches in the orchard back home, so why not here? I leaned forward and wrapped my hands around the tightrope, lifted my left leg and placed my foot on the tightrope behind my hands. I extended myself into an upside down U then slowly and carefully lifted both legs up into the air. I became a Y.

"Bea..." Jacques was already across and on to the platform, preparing for the dismount I'd missed the night I came to see the Great Romanini. "Bea..." he hissed again, "what are you doing?"

I laughed. This was the best day of my life. I walked, on my hands of course, to the end of the tightrope, manoeuvred myself, a little clumsily Jacques said later, on to the platform, returned to my feet and saw I'd missed the grand finale again.

Jacques was already on the net, bowing deeply in the direction of the rani.

My head was buzzing – and not just because I'd been walking upside down. I raised my arms and launched myself off the platform, as if I was diving into our pool in the jungle.

"Weeeeeee!" I yelled as I fell, tucking myself into a ball in time to bounce into the net and hurtle back into the air. I landed on my back and lay there looking in wonder at the tightrope so high above. I was up there – I did it. I did it.

"What were you doing, you stupid girl..." Jacques

was standing over me. He put a hand out and started pulling me to my feet. "Never, ever do that – never change a routine once you leave the floor of the ring. Never."

His eyes were ablaze. "Never, never, never – you could have killed yourself and that would have got us all killed, you..."

"But I didn't," I said and flung my arms around him.

For a cloudy moment after I opened my eyes, I thought I was home again, back in Glen Laddich. There it was…

"Peeeew, peeeew!"

The cry of the buzzard. I blinked and rubbed my eyes. Sunshine streamed in through the window. It wasn't a buzzard. Every morning it caught me out. I rolled off the charpoy, the small bed on which I'd spent each night since we'd been brought to the rani's distant fort, and peered sleepily out the window.

There it was, riding the updraught of warm air, wings spread, razor-sharp eyes searching the ground far below for prey. A kite, a red kite, red to match the stone of our new fort home.

My room was second-but-one from the top of a thin

tower. The fort was built on the edge of a precipice and the view from the window was huge, a vast swathe of India stretched out below like a landscape painting. If the British army was to march on the rani's fortress I would have a grandstand view of their progress, because somewhere over the horizon was Agra.

It was why there were lookouts in the room above. Below, me, Jacques and Pin shared a room. The rooms were connected by a series of ladders that poked through hatches in the middle of the floor. It meant I was woken constantly through the night by the lookouts' noisy comings and goings. When I tried to shush them they blew raspberries and called me Missie Baba, little girl. In return I threw the best of the insults Private Coombe had taught me. They didn't know what my curses meant but they got the gist, hooting with laughter in response.

I yawned. I'd been woken three times in the night and now the kite had finished off my attempts at sleep. I could rest this afternoon, down in the fort garden, find a shady spot near the fountain, next to the rani's small temple, and doze off listening to the screeching of the peacocks.

In the mornings we were expected to practise.

That's what the rani's minister told us when we arrived, bones still rattling after a long and jarring journey on their elephant. We were to be the rani's acrobats, to perform at banquets and other feasts and celebrations.

A tightrope and a couple of swings had been set up under Jacques' supervision above one of the courtyards where the rani liked to practise her wrestling and sword fighting. I watched her once. It was like she was dancing; her feet were so quick, her blade flashing in the sun. Close my eyes and I can see her still, a breastplate strapped over her robes, darting forward, raising her sword, the clash of colliding steel echoing around the courtyard followed by her cry of triumph. She made others brave; she made me brave.

The tightrope was tied between two balconies while the swings hung from the balustrades. Every morning a small crowd gathered to watch: servants, soldiers, even some of the rani's ministers and advisers (who were happy to advise but less happy to follow their own advice and go out and fight alongside the rani).

Pin had taken it on himself to be our ringmaster and made me and Jacques wait until the morning's audience had gathered before announcing us. He'd usher the watchers into position with cries of *Roll up, roll up*.

"You are privileged to be here, my lords, ladies and gentlemen, to see one of the wonders of the circus world, a world so wonderful you might wonder if your very eyes are deceiving you – but they are not, because seeing is to believe in..." and here his voice would rise as he lifted his arms "...the Great Romanini and Julietteeeerrrr!"

He would switch languages depending on his mood, or where his words took him. Sometimes we understood nothing of what he said, apart from the end. That was always the same... lift the arms and the volume... "...the Great Romanini and Julietteeeerrrr!"

Jacques wasn't best pleased about it and although I secretly liked being announced as Julietterrrr I also felt guilty for having claimed Vette's Big Top name. It was a spur of the moment thing, a keeping-us-alive spur of the moment thing. If I'd told the rani my real name was Beatrice Spelling and my uncle was Theophilus Campbell, magistrate of Agra, then our chances of survival would have been slimmer than a page of pocket Bible paper.

So Juliette I remained to all in the rani's fort, which was hard because it's easy to forget who you're supposed to be when you're being someone you're not. On Pin's nod, I'd appear on the balcony and say "Romanini, Romanini, wherefore art thou the Great Romanini?"

Whereupon Jacques would leap from the opposite balcony and begin whatever routine we were practising that day. At first Jacques refused but Pin was persuasive.

"This William Shakespeare was a great, great writer I believe. I read…"

"Yes, yes," said Jacques.

"Yes, so he wrote that… let me think, yes, 'all the world is a stage'. And that is right because we must put on a show all the time for the rani's people – make them come to love us and then they'll protect us, so we'll be safe. We can have a good life here. What is it you say, Jacques? The show must go on. You see?"

Jacques nodded doubtfully.

"All for one and one for all," asserted Pin, as he had begun to do when we disagreed with one of his suggestions. I opened my mouth to say something, then closed it.

Days turned into weeks. We practised and the small crowds grew and one day it occurred to me that the perfect time for the British to launch an attack would be during our performance.

The audience were crammed in beneath the tightrope. They ooooed and ahhhed and clapped and cheered and with each day that passed, Pin's ringmaster costume became ever more elaborate. He wore a white turban with a large gold star sewn on the front and a golden sash slung across his skinny body, which was covered by a flowing white robe on which he had sewn more gold stars. The look was set off by a pair of golden slippers that curved upwards at the end with a small bell dangling from each tip. It meant he jingled when he walked.

"You look ridiculous," said Jacques. "Where's your flying carpet?"

Pin laughed. "It's all for show, Jacques, all for show – beneath I'm Pin, always Pingali. When I was a servant – a slave – for the British, I was Pingali underneath, always Pingali. Now I'm a ringmaster to the rani's people but still Pin to you and Pin to me, always Pingali."

He clapped his hands. "Now, places – the show it must..."

"Oui, oui," said Jacques and shrugged at me.

I couldn't imagine life without Jacques and Pin. They'd become brothers, my brothers. Losing Tonton had pushed us even closer together.

But they weren't replacements for George. I was thinking about him more and more. He was my blood brother after all. How he would have grown since I last saw him. With every day that passed, the feeling grew inside me, nagged at me; I had to find him, had to find my missing brother. As his older sister, I owed that to him and Mother. Yes, it was fun (and safe) living in the fort and being part of a circus act – we'd proved ourselves the Acrobats of Agra – but we were still trapped. Just like we'd been trapped in the fort at Agra even if this was a golden cage we were shut in.

Pin told me we were closer to Hulla than we'd been at Agra. He said he'd ask around for any news of the station. Many of the stations had been attacked and burnt to the ground; in return the advancing British soldiers were destroying village after village. The longer this war went on the crueller it was becoming – the British were taking a terrible revenge for the rebellion. Was there any chance George might have survived all the killing and bloodshed?

"I must do it slowly and extra, extra carefully," explained Pin. "We cannot run the risk of someone thinking I'm a spy because I'm asking about British stations. The rani has given us her blessing but there are others who mistrust everyone who is not Indian – just as your British don't trust anyone at all who is Indian – and they will seize any chance to condemn us to a terrible fate."

It chewed at me. I had to find George. You understand? I missed my family. I tried not to miss them – because they're gone, Mother and Father. They're not coming back and for a lot of the time I don't think of them. Then, out of nowhere, they come back, inside me, and it hurts. I want to feel Mother put her arms around me. I wish I could remember that. I do miss her, and every day her face becomes harder and harder to see. But George… him I could still get to see, actually in front of me, flesh and blood, my flesh and blood.

It ate at me so much that one morning I lost my footing on the tightrope and fell. I couldn't concentrate; my mind had gone leapy again, darting here, there and everywhere. Fortunately the courtyard was packed, so my landing was soft with the crowd acting as my safety net.

"I must go and find George," I told Pin and Jacques as they bent over me.

"No," said Pin, "you cannot."

"I must."

It turned out Pin was right (as usual). Early the next morning, before the sun was out of bed, I packed a small bag, left a note for Pin and Jacques – promising I would return for them as soon as I found my brother and we could all live together as one happy family (with no aunts or uncles to tell us what to do!) – and climbed quietly down the ladders.

The first guard on the gate shook his head. I turned to the second and began pleading. He shook his head as well.

"Nobody can leave the fort without the permission of the rani."

"Well, she's not here and I'm sure if she was she would let me, it's important, very important."

The second guard shook his head again.

"Go away, Missie," said the first one.

It was hopeless. I turned and trudged back up towards the tower.

"We'll come and watch you later, Missie," shouted the first one. "We never miss a morning watching you walk on air."

I glanced back and the guard waved, a big smile on his face.

The boys weren't smiling when I poked my head through the hatch into their room. They'd read the note.

"What were you thinking?" scolded Pin. "I told you it's dangerous, very dangerous – for all of us."

A tear, fat and wet, rolled down my cheek.

"I just want to find him… to see him, hold him."

Jacques put his hands out; I took them and he pulled me close. I sobbed into his shoulder.

Later that morning I stood on the balcony and saw the faces of the two guards among the crowd. They waved up at me. I gave a small nod of recognition in return.

I wasn't angry with them, the guards. I was angry with all of them, all of them together, everyone, the Indians for rebelling, the British for causing it,

Uncle Theo, the governor, the soldiers in red coats, Aunt Constance for being such a stickler for the rules, Primrose for being so prim. And above all my parents, Mother and Father, my dead mother and father, for coming here in the first place, for leaving me with Grannie and then not being around to stop me being taken away from Grannie, and most of all for not being here when I needed them, like I'd never needed them in my whole, entire life.

What about *me*?

I lay in bed that night and sighed and sighed as I tossed and turned. I wanted to find George. I *had* to find George. And if Pin and Jacques wouldn't come with me, I would have to go by myself and sort things out with them later. Which I knew I could because me, Pin and Jacques had a bond that could not be broken. We might have a furious row first but it would be all right in the end.

Wouldn't it?

I sighed once more and turned on to my back.

It would, wouldn't it?

Would it?

At some point in that long night I decided to make

a rope. I would take the tightrope and any other rope I could find, tie it together, add clothes and bedclothes, anything, lower it out the window and slide down it to escape. Yes, I thought, and closed my eyes: a good plan.

In the morning I bounced over to the window and felt the bounce leave me as I looked out and down and down and realised I would never find a rope long enough to reach the ground.

I stared out the window. In the distance a cloud of dust was galloping across the plain. "Oh," I said and rushed to the ladder that led up to the lookouts' room. "They're coming!" I yelled. There was no reply so I climbed the ladder and poked my head through the hatch.

Two lookouts were asleep on charpoys, a third was asleep by the window.

"WAKE UP!"

The two men on the charpoys leapt up and grabbed their weapons, the other rushed for the alarm bell, leaning out the window to start clanging the bell as hard as he could.

We slid down the ladders; I collected the boys and we rushed for the ramparts overlooking the main gate.

A crowd of the rani's soldiers, ministers and servants were already crammed onto them by the time we got there.

"Here," said Pin and led us to the second wall, where another set of ramparts looked down on the outer wall and main gate. We joined a line of soldiers, who recognised us and patted us on the back in between loading their guns.

"Look," shouted one, switching attention back to the force approaching the fort. "It's Her Highness, it's the rani!"

The huge gates were pushed open and the drawbridge lowered to cheers from the soldiers on the ramparts.

"All hail, the rani!"

"Hurray for the great rani – crusher of the British, freer of Jhansi."

Pin translated for us. Then came a chant that needed no explanation.

"Rani! rani! rani!"

Soon everyone was yelling her name as she led her army back into the fort, hooves echoing off the walls as she galloped beneath the gatehouse on her familiar chestnut mount.

It was infectious. "Rani! rani!" I shouted along with the rest of them.

For once she did not look immaculate, her white robes covered by the dust of the plains. She pulled away her face mask as she entered the fort and waved to her soldiers and ministers. Her sharp eyes ran along the ramparts and for a moment found me.

It was just for a moment but enough to feel the strength of her look, the rani's eyes appraising each person and asking, "You are with me, aren't you?"

"Yes," I said. "I am."

"What?" said Pin, breaking off from his chants of the rani's name.

"Oh, nothing." But it wasn't nothing because in that moment I decided what to do – the answer was staring me in the face. I had to be true to the rani. I would tell the rani everything, admit I wasn't Juliette, the French acrobat, admit I was Beatrice Spelling, niece of a hated British magistrate, and plead with the rani to let me go and find my brother, my wee George (taking the boys with me because they were my family as well). If anyone would understand, it would be the rani. I was sure of that.

Pin didn't think so and Jacques backed him up.

"No," said Pin, "over my dead body."

"Non," said Jacques, and added a few more for emphasis, "non, non, non."

"She will kill us – enough of her ministers already think we're spies. Tell her who you really are and we'll all be hanging from the ramparts before you can say 'tiffin time is time for tea'."

"What?"

"The governor's children... their English nanny used to say it when... doesn't matter, what matters is you're not going to tell the rani anything of the sort. I'll tie you up if I have to."

He didn't mean it. I was sure of that. Pretty sure, and anyway he never had the chance. That evening we were called to perform before the rani. The ministers had planned a huge banquet but the rani ordered the food taken to her soldiers who had been on the march for days. Anything left was to be given to the servants in the fort.

Pin swore he saw steam coming out the Chief Minister's ears when the rani instructed him to take the food away. Instead, the rani declared, 'We will eat simply, we are at war so there is no time for feasts when my people outside these walls are starving and dying.'

I listened to the rani's orders. She would understand. My mind was made up. I was going to tell her.

Pin eyed me anxiously as we waited to start the performance. The rani stood on the balcony where Jacques would begin. She stepped aside to let him out when Pin, down below in the courtyard, announced the Great Romanini.

The performance went without a hitch. I was nervous before it began – Jacques told me he was as well, always. "If you lose your nerves before you begin, you lose your performance," he said.

Once I stepped out on the tightrope the butterflies flapped away into the night sky and, despite knowing what I was going to do afterwards and what that might mean, my concentration was ferocious. Because I'd found something I loved, and something I was getting good at. Very good actually, although I would never say that within anyone's earshot.

I didn't put a foot wrong. Even Jacques, who demanded perfection on the rope, gave me a quick hug afterwards. I think he knew what I was going to do because he knew me. When you live with someone in a dangerous time you get to understand them far quicker than normal. And despite his earlier objections I knew he was not going to try to stop me – because he would have done the same thing if he were me.

Later that evening I left the boys wolfing down their share of the banquet the rani sent up to the tower and made my way to the great hall. I peered around huge doors. The room was full of men sitting at long tables eating dhal and chapattis with puffed rice as a sweet(ish) treat. They did not look happy with their dinner. The wooden throne at the far end of the room was empty.

"She's in the garden." It was one of the guards who had turned me away from the gates. "I am just taking this to her."

He held a plate piled high with banquet food, the colours of the rainbow, orange, green, red. "Follow me, stay close."

When we reached the garden, the guard handed me the plate. "Take it, give it to her, it'll get you past the moaning ministers."

He stepped in front of me and raised his voice. "Make way, make way – this is for Her Highness."

The gathering of ministers, commanders and maids of honour parted and I was ushered through. The rani sat on a stone seat carved into the far wall. It was my favourite spot, where I liked to come and doze and daydream in the heat of the afternoons.

I stepped forward, dropped to one knee, bowed my head and offered the plate to the rani.

"Look at me," said the rani. I half raised my head and lifted my eyes to peer at this young woman – younger than Miss Goodenough – who held the power of life and death over me, the boys and who knows how many thousands of others.

All it would take was a flick of the rani's fingers and my life would be over. This was a tightrope act in which I could not afford the tiniest mistake. But this time I did not feel nervous. I *knew* the rani would understand.

"What is it child?"

"I need to tell you something and I need to beg for your forgiveness and I need to beg for your help..."

"Apologies, your Highness, I will get rid of her..." One of her commanders, a man with the curliest moustache I'd ever seen, stepped forward and placed a hand on my shoulder.

The rani raised one of her own, and waved him away. "Take the plate down to the guards on the gate," she instructed the commander, and once it was done turned her attention to me.

"Come closer," she said. "Tell me, my child."

So I did as the rani ordered.

She did not interrupt as I spoke, hesitantly at first but then everything just poured out. I told her it all, even about Tonton, and when I finished I bowed my head and closed my eyes. There – it was done.

I opened my eyes and looked up at her. The rani swung her gaze up into the clear night sky, catching sight of the stars. She sighed.

"The magistrate of Agra, your uncle… you know what each and every one of my ministers and commanders would advise me to do. We must kill our enemies. That is what war demands – and we are at war, your people and my people."

She was still looking at the stars. I watched her through my eyelashes.

"Do you know," she said quietly, "what your people have done to my people, in this war and for many,

many years before that, men like your uncle? We are in a fight to the death. They are coming here, your people's soldiers... we don't know when but they will come and they will come for me and all my people. They will show us no mercy. They will kill us all if they can, every man, woman and child.

"*Mena Jhansi nahin denge*..." In her own language, her voice was suddenly fierce. "Never will I give up my people to the British... never will I give up my Jhansi."

She paused and sighed once more. She looked down at me and shook her head.

"My people come to watch you and they don't see a British girl, they just see you, a girl, and the boy... they stand there, look up at you and marvel. They all want to walk on air like you do – we all want to walk on air."

Her gaze returned to the night sky, a sky that went on forever.

"Sometimes I wish I could be up there and never have to look down. Never have to see again what a mess this world has become. So much death, so much destruction. It has to be done, the British have to be thrown from all India. And it has to be done at the point of a sword, for how else could the British be made to go, for yours are a greedy people.

"No… it can still be done with honour. There has been too much cruelty… too much. No more, no more…"

Her voice dropped to a whisper as she finished. It seemed as if she was talking more to herself than to me. She gestured for one of her maids and instructed her in a voice too low for me to catch. The maid bowed and hurried away. She turned to the curly-moustached commander.

"Fetch me the two boys, bring them here at once."

I bowed my head once more and focussed on the grass. My left leg was beginning to ache from kneeling, I longed to stand up and stretch. Like my mind, my body wasn't made for keeping still. I swallowed. What had I done?

There was a commotion and Pin and Jacques were pushed through. Pin lost his footing and fell, sprawling on the grass, his knee leaving a dark mark.

The rani stepped towards him and lifted him to his knees. Pin joined Jacques and me in bowing before her. My left knee was beginning to shake.

The maid returned, holding a pot.

"Tomorrow morning you will leave my fort – you will have my mark on you. For as long as that lasts you have my protection."

The maid handed her the pot and lifted my head. The rani dipped a finger in the pot and smeared something on my forehead. The maid and rani did the same to the boys, the maid tilting their heads up and the rani pressing her thumb against their foreheads.

The rani gave the pot back to the maid and stepped between me and Jacques; as she did she touched her hand ever so slightly on my head.

"Take them back to the tower – they leave at dawn."

I remained bowed but turned my head to see the crowd part for the rani. It closed behind her and I never saw her again. I owe her my life.

I hurried towards the rising sun. We'd left the rani's fort in darkness, dawn a hint on the horizon and as the sun began to climb into the sky so our pace quickened. I was impatient, I wanted to get the journey over and done with, find George and then... well, "then" would take care of itself.

Our plan was much as before, push on until the day heated up and then walk again at night. This time though we were better prepared and better equipped.

"Once more unto the breach," said Pin.

I glanced back. "What?"

"It's Shakespeare," said Pin.

"Oh," I said.

"Henry the Fifth," he added.

This was beginning to sound like one of Miss

Goodenough's history lessons. I turned away from him and fixed my gaze down the road.

I'd told Pin I would understand if he preferred to stay with the rani. He seemed at home in the fort, and I think he felt he belonged somewhere at long last – somewhere he might in time be himself rather than Pin the Chameleon. But he wouldn't hear of it, spoke of his dhama, his duty, to me and Jacques, and the memory of Tonton.

"As my grandfather told me, it was Arjuna's duty to fight, to never give up. Krishna persuaded him he must fight and I know I must go with you. That's my dhama… and besides I've already left a sweet treat for Ganesha so that he will come with us as well."

The rani had sent one of her officers to instruct us on what lay between the fort and Hulla. He lectured us like Miss Goodenough and I wrote down notes as if I were in one of her classes. Pin said he'd remember the directions but I wanted to be sure… *when you reach the tree that points two ways turn north… take care at the crossing point before the next village, there are Jats there who often set an ambush – they are not to be trusted…*

The officer told us about the different armies and

bandits we might bump into – there was a mish-mash group of deserters and other flotsam and jetsam terrorising the countryside. It more or less came down to one instruction: *Avoid everybody apart from the rani's men because they're all dangerous, including the British. They will shoot you first then ask who you jolly well are.*

After the officer was done, wishing us a safe journey because if the rani trusts you, you are to be trusted, another soldier appeared with three packs, each containing a thin sleeping mat, rolled-up and tied to the bottom, small sacks of dried fruit, flasks of water, and a turban. "Soak it and it keeps you cool while you march," explained the soldier. They also held three of the white-topped and baggy-trousered uniforms the rani's soldiers wore. Mine had come from one of her handmaidens but I still had to roll up the trousers, and the belt came in handy for keeping them up.

He gave us a tulwa, a dagger and three pistols. "Do you know how to load them?" he asked the boys and was surprised when I said I did. "I will teach the boys," I said.

I could feel my pistol, thrust in my belt, the butt rubbing against my stomach and growing heavier with each step. I thought about throwing it away – if we got into a situation where we needed it, it would probably be too late to use it – but decided to keep it. There was a comfort in being armed for this dangerous journey.

We made good progress, the fort slipping down the horizon behind us. It was good to be on the move again. I lifted my chin and sang, an old, old song Grannie taught me…

Twas in the early morning, when we marched awa
And O but the captain he was sorry-o
The drums they did beat o'er the bonnie braes o'Gight
And the band played the bonnie lass of Fyvie-o.

I used to sing it setting off for the top of Glen Laddich, my piece in my bag for a summer's day adventure, imagining I was the bonnie lass of Fyvie-o. For this adventure I had two captains with me. I stopped halfway through the last verse when I remembered the captain died for the bonnie lass.

For the first two days we saw no one. Not a soul. There was no shortage of signs mankind had been this way: more ruined villages, deserted apart from stray dogs and the shambling shapes of vultures filling themselves on things that didn't bear a closer look.

Early on the third day the road brought us to a large tree. Three people were sitting beneath its branches – it looked a good place to duck out of the sun. From a distance there was something peculiar about them. We approached cautiously; I rested a wary hand on the butt of the pistol. I wondered if I should load it.

"Urgh," said Pin, who was a little way ahead of us, and covered his mouth. "Don't look."

Too late. The three were people no longer, bodies picked clean by the vultures. The skeletons sat and watched us hurry by.

On the fifth day, a group of horsemen surrounded us. We saw them from far away. There was nowhere for us to go, nothing to do but wait until they caught up with us. I loaded the pistol and held it by my side.

They drew their swords when they saw us. Dust swirled around us as they circled. I think my knees might have started shaking. Then one of them caught sight of the marks on our foreheads, the rani's golden X. In a flash swords were returned to scabbards.

"You are blessed by the Golden Queen," said their leader and ordered his men to give us food and water before sending us on our way with hearty cheers.

The following day brought us to the tree that points two ways. "This way," said Pin as I paused to study my notes. Further on, we waited until darkness to cross the ford, the one we'd been warned about, and took a cautious detour around the dangerous village, keeping a sharp eye out for Jats and ambushes.

Crossing the ford meant we'd left the rani's lands so we washed the gold crosses from our foreheads. We were beyond the rani's reach; she'd done all she could for us.

The country became hillier and when we turned on to a larger road we knew we were close.

"There," said Pin, pointing to a cluster of houses in a pleasant tree-dotted valley. Even from this distance we could see the houses were not homes any more. More skeletons; this time skeletons of the buildings they had once been.

The Collector's bungalow was the largest. Somehow the wooden gate, a wooden gate that looked as if it belonged in front of a picture-book English cottage, remained intact. It clicked shut behind us.

I stared at what lay in front of us.

The bungalow had been built to look like a country cottage; now it was roofless, its windows smashed and black scars left by flames marking its walls. A perfect circle decorated the front door, where a cannon ball had come knocking. The walls were peppered with bullet holes.

"You should wait here," said Jacques, putting a hand on my arm. Pin mounted the three wide steps that led to the front door and pushed. The door fell to the ground with a crash, raising a puff of ashes and dust.

"No," I said and walked into Aunt Celia's house… George's home.

The boys followed me. I drew the pistol and held

it in front of me as I walked from room to room. The house had been looted, much of what was left smashed to pieces. There was no sign of George.

"Which is good," pointed out Pin, "I think that means he's still alive Bea, otherwise we would be looking at his skeleton – they would have killed them all here, there would be bodies everywhere..."

Jacques shot him a look. "Oh, sorry," said Pin. "I didn't mean, well, you know I…"

A line of red ants marched determinedly across the floor and into a small room leading off the main bedroom.

"Ants," said Pin, "always busy, always work to do."

I shoved the pistol back into my belt and followed the ants into the small room, the nursery.

An overturned cot sat in the middle of the room, next to it a nursing chair that had lost its legs. And there it was, lying in the corner, dirty and abandoned.

I scooped it up and held it tight. My legs wobbled and I slumped against the wall before slipping to the floor and curling up in the corner, eyes squeezed shut.

"What is it?" asked Jacques. Pin crouched down beside me. I knew it was him without opening my eyes.

"What is it?" said Jacques. Gently, Pin opened my hand; I didn't try to stop him. A dusty piece of cloth fell to the floor.

"What is it?" Jacques tried again. Pin picked it up. No, it wasn't a piece of cloth.

"Baby George…" I said. I sniffed and took it from Pin. "It's Baby George's rabbit, I made it for him before he went to India…"

I pushed myself up and wiped my nose with my sleeve, adding another sniff to be sure. I held Rabbit by one ear so they could see: a cloth for its body, a tuft of a tail and four legs attached to the cloth beneath a long-eared head with a stitched smile. I went back into the bedroom.

The last time I'd seen Rabbit had been on the dock in Glasgow – the last time I'd seen my parents and Baby George. Mother kissed me, Father patted my head and I'd pressed Rabbit into Baby George's crib, a rabbit I'd spent every day sewing since Mother told me about India because it stopped me from crying.

"Now, be a brave girl, Beatrice," Father had said. He never called me Bea. "No blubbing."

The last words he spoke to me.

I sniffed again and twitched my shoulder, remembering Grannie's hand there as we stood on the dock and watched the ship sail down the Clyde. She had a fast coach on hand to hurry us around the coast so I could get one last look at the ship before it headed into the Atlantic Ocean. We'd stood on the beach at Gourock; I ran to the very edge of the waves and waved and waved at the ship. The great sails fluttered in the strengthening wind but no one waved back.

"Gone," I said, then whisked the pistol out of my belt. "Stay still or I shoot."

The boys spun round. I hoped the old man hesitating by the doorway wouldn't realise the pistol wasn't loaded.

He raised his hands. "No, no," he said and shook his head.

"Who are you?" said Pin.

"Come," said the man and gestured for them to follow. "Not safe here, much danger, come."

He turned his back on us and shuffled out of the

house. We followed, pausing at the front door to scan the garden and the road beyond. There was no sign of life.

"Keep that pistol pointed at him," said Pin and I realised he didn't know it wasn't loaded either.

We followed the man behind the house and along a path leading through a cluster of trees to another oddly intact gate. There was something reassuring about the click of it closing behind us even amid all this chaos. Beyond lay a small hut, untouched by the destruction across the rest of the station. I noticed a small but familiar elephant head carved into the frame of the doorway.

The man lifted a thin curtain and beckoned us inside. I was still clutching Rabbit in my other hand.

"Must get you out of sight," he said. "Quick, quick."

It was gloomy inside. I blinked to accustom my eyes to the dark. I still held the pistol ready.

"No, no, put it away." The voice came from a charpoy in the corner. I peered towards it. An old woman sat up.

"My wife, she was the chota sahib's ayah, I'm afraid she is not well… ever since they were taken…" The man let the curtain fall back, removing most of the little light from the hut's single room.

"Who was taken... where? Who's Chota? What's..."

"Bea, take a breath... the ayah's right, put the pistol away – you must not enter someone's home waving a pistol, it's not right at all."

I glared at Pin, my mood catching the gloom of our surroundings. I shoved the pistol back into my belt and squatted down facing the old woman.

"Where are they?"

"Chota sahib," said Pin. "Little Master; she looked after the master's boy – she looked after your brother..."

"Pinnnn..." I wished he'd be quiet.

"Sit, please, sit and I'll fetch you some water."

Pin turned and gave a little bow in response to the man. "Patience – do as he asks," he whispered to me. "They're taking a huge risk having us in their house – we must remember our manners and respect their customs."

"Manners! My baby brother is..."

Jacques laid a calming arm on mine. He was becoming my calmer-downer (everyone needs a calmer-downer), and he was good at it.

I said nothing and sat down cross-legged in front of the charpoy. The man brought our water and perched himself on the end of the bed. I took a large gulp, then another.

"We knew they would come, everyone knew they would come. The Collector decided..."

"What about George? What about the chota?" I interrupted.

The man raised a finger curved with age and continued. "The Collector decided to fight. They would barricade themselves in the Collector's house; I think he imagined he was an Englishman in a castle. Everyone left... we hid, and we saw. They came, early one morning..."

His voice trailed off.

"Who came?" prompted Pin.

"Men... rebels... many, many of them..."

"What happened to George... where's George... tell me," I snapped another interruption.

"When the Collector wouldn't come out they set fire to the roof and fired a canon through the door. They came out. The Collector first, Mrs Collector... they marched them to the next valley, I followed, hiding, there were shots and screams...

I couldn't see it all… I ran back here, I was very afraid…"

"What about George?" I said, feeling the blood drain from my face. My head span.

The old man shook his head. "When they had gone we waited, a long while because we were scared. We did not dare to go outside. It's hard to think of others when you are terrified for yourself."

"My brother… George?"

The woman leaned forward and reached out a hand. I took it and the woman placed her other one on top and held my hand tight.

"Your brother, your beautiful brother. He is a sunbeam, lighting up life," she said and squeezed my hand even more tightly.

"He's dead… is he?"

"It was dark and more came, men, bad men, red coats, red faces and others…"

The woman made a hacking sound and spat on the floor, making me jump with the unexpected aggression of her action. "Budmache," she hissed. "Goonda."

"British?"

The man shook his head. "Yes, but different, they have run away from the red coats… we heard the boy scream – he'd been hiding in the bungalow but they found him and they took him…"

"He's alive!" It came out as a screech. I snatched my hand from the woman's grip and pressed it against my mouth. Because I wanted to scream.

Pin put an arm around me. Jacques matched him from the other side.

"He is alive, isn't he?"

"He is," said the old man. "But they have him – they found us and they left us alive to tell the British when they come back, if a ransom is not paid they will…" He swallowed and looked up at me.

"No," I said. "That won't happen. We will find him and we will take him home."

I shrugged off the boys' arms and stood up.

"We will won't we?"

And they both, without a second thought, nodded.

22

Chama – that was the old man's name – shook his head. He did a lot of that, headshaking.

"They are budmache, bad men – kill without a second thought, men, women, children. You are children." He was still shaking his head. His wife, Chaneshwari, joined in. They were scared, scared by what they had seen, scared of what was going to happen to them since their world had been tipped upside down and everything had fallen out.

"Will you help us?"

Perhaps I shouldn't have asked them but we needed all the help we could get. The deserters had taken over a large old fort deeper in the hills, two days' journey from Hulla. That's where they would be holding George, according to Chama, so that's where we were going to go to rescue him. Whatever it took.

"All for one and..." I said and the boys completed our pact, chanting the words together. "One for all."

Chama was still shaking his head when we set off for the fort. Chaneshwari (we called her Chana – Chana and Chama) persuaded him they would accompany us. She took her husband by the arm and led him away from their home.

"We are coming to save the boy," she informed us. Chama shook his head but made no move to turn back and was soon directing us along our journey.

But how were we going to save George? Chama was right. We were children, and two old people. We had three pistols.

"And me," said Pin.

We'd reached the fort and were lying in a row on the edge of the forest. Ahead of us the ground had been cleared to give the fort's defenders a clear shot at any attackers. We could see two of them lolling by the gate, armed to the teeth with a musket, pistol and tulwa each. One wore a dirty red coat, the other a shirt that might once have been white and might once have had arms.

"We have my mind – I will think of something, do not worry."

I glanced round at Pin. Sometimes I didn't know whether he was being serious or not. He nodded at me, a determined look on his face.

"I will," he insisted.

We slithered backwards and retreated into the deep cover of the forest. To where Chama and Chana lent against the broad trunk of a peepal tree. They looked tired.

"In there," began Chama and pointed to the fort, "they are not like us, not like other men. They… they have powers, dark powers I think."

"Ganesha will protect us," declared Pin.

"I have seen them – with my own eyes… there is one, a large man with a round head, this man can make fire come from his mouth. He is like a human dragon…"

"Puffff," said Pin, in a tone that left no doubt where he stood on Chama's claims of a human dragon.

Jacques sat up. He'd been lying back, hands behind his head, staring at the snatches of cloud and blue sky visible through the treetops. Sometimes I thought I saw Tonton in the clouds. Perhaps Jacques was looking for her up there.

"Fire comes from his mouth?"

Chama nodded. "He breathes fire, they say…"

"They say? Did you see him?"

"They said he was a big, big man, not an Indian and not a Britisher and fire…"

"Yes, but did you see him – with your own two eyes, Chama?"

"Well, I myself did not but I have heard…"

Jacques lay back again with a sigh.

"What is it Jacques?"

"Nothing," he said. "I just thought… oh, nothing, it really doesn't matter."

Chama shook his head. "Much danger, much danger." He shook his head again. "There might be a way into the fort, the north wall has been crumbling for many years, the forest wants it back so it is trying to invade the fort but very dangerous, very, very dangerous." One more shake and he was done.

"You know the fort?"

"Oh yes, when I was a young man I was a servant

here when the Nawab used it for hunting parties. He used to ride a tiger around the garden, but that is all gone now, long, long gone."

I looked at Jacques, who swallowed and glanced away into the trees. Chama picked up a stick and began to draw in the dust. "Here is the entrance, into a courtyard and there are..."

It took him several minutes to draw his plan of the fort and explain where everything was as he recalled it. "My memory is not always strong," he said.

"Knowing half something can be dangerous," said Pin. "It says that..."

"In the Mahabharata," interrupted Chama. "The great story."

"You know the great story, Grandfather's story?"

"If you proceed to war treating equally joy and sorrow, gain and loss, victory and defeat, you do not sin. So said Vishnu to..."

"Arjuna. He's my hero, Arjuna. Vishnu told Arjuna why he must fight and the Pandavas fought the Kauravas and they won despite the Pandavas having 100,000 war elephants and the Kauravas a whole 200,000 war elephants and many, many more soldiers than Arjuna and the Pandavas. The Pandavas had less and they won. 18 days the battle raged and they won… didn't they Grandfather?"

Chama smiled at Pin. "Something like that, boy, something like that."

"War elephants… does that mean elephants with armour? Imagine if we just had one war elephant we could smash down the fort walls and charge in and rescue George just like that." I could picture it, me and Pin riding the elephant, cheering as it charged into the fort, swatting aside with its mighty trunk the men who held George …

"This is no time for daydreaming, Bea," interrupted Pin. "No, we'll have to be cunning, like Ganesha's mouse – the mouse can go places the elephant can't. Brains can beat brawn. The mouse can go unseen – we must get away without them seeing us go; disappear into thin air, otherwise they will chase us and we're doomed if that happens."

"Why don't me and Jacques take a walk around the fort, see what we can see?" I suggested, keen to show I could contribute more than a fantasy to Pin's plan. "Knowing something's better than knowing nothing."

Pin stuck his tongue out at me. His grandfather hadn't taught him that.

The north side, it turned out, was even more crumbled than Chama suggested. It had been years since he'd last seen the fort and the forest had been busy.

Trees as tall as the walls and a thick covering of undergrowth had grown up to the north wall. Vines snaked up it, as if the forest monkeys had hung them there to make their entrance to the fort easier. There was a covered turret on either corner with narrow slits for windows. We squatted in the undergrowth and watched for what seemed an age. Nothing moved.

"Shall we?" I whispered. I don't know why I whispered, but sometimes you feel you should. I had a feeling about the fort, and the men inside, the men we had to outwit, that made me drop my voice.

A narrow path had been hacked along the bottom of the wall, just wide enough for a man to walk along, probably for a guard doing his rounds, so we would have to be vigilant. The vines scaling the wall had been left untouched and it was easy for Jacques to climb them. And me. But not a fully-grown adult – a child's weight was the most they would hold.

We reached the top pretty quickly and peeked over. Like the wall, this end of the fort was falling into ruin.

There was no sign of life. Inside we could see a couple of buildings as Chama described. The one nearest us looked unused. The flat roof of the other was visible beyond. In front of us there was a walkway around the walls. It looked ready to crumble at anything but the touch of the smallest foot.

Behind us, somewhere in the forest, a monkey screeched and I jumped. For a moment I let go of the vine. I slithered down, hands scrambling for a hold. The skin tore off my knees. I let out a moan of pain and grabbed a hold. I was breathing heavily and could feel sweat running down my back. My head pounded. I needed to get down.

"Bea?" wondered Jacques, but I kept going down.

When he joined me on the ground I was leaning over, hands on knees.

"Bea... what's the matter?"

Jacques bent over next to me, a concerned hand on my back. It meant neither of us saw him coming, and that might have cost us our lives.

What spared us was the simple snapping of a twig. For a big man – and he was massive, much bigger than he'd seemed in the ring – he moved so quietly but his weight was more than enough to break the twig with a clean snap.

"What..." said Jacques glancing round.

Jacques, so used to split-second decisions, reacted quickest. He pushed me and dived. I felt the air part as I fell and the club swooshed down and thudded into the ground just where I'd been standing.

I kept rolling, the forest tumbling upside down around me. I heard a grunt from the man, then a growl. I scrambled to my feet and glanced over my shoulder.

Our attacker had heaved his club over his shoulders again, preparing to bring it down. His eyes were focussed on Jacques, who was flat on his back. The man's left foot was on Jacques' right ankle, pinning him to the ground.

"Huuuurrrggggh," said the man as he lifted his club as high as he could. Jacques wriggled in vain. He was trapped.

"Noooooo," I yelled, launching myself at him, a fly attacking an elephant.

"KAMALLLLLL..."

Jacques' shout was desperate, shrill and finished the split second I crashed into the man's tummy. It was like leaping into a brick wall. A sharp pain cracked down my neck and into my shoulder. I don't think the man even flinched. He swatted at me with one hand. I slid down his leg and landed on Jacques. My head was spinning.

"KAMALLL..."

The man had two hands on the club again and

lifted it once more, eyes swivelling between me and Jacques, as if deciding whom he would bludgeon first.

"It's me, Kamal, c'est moi… look…" Jacques made one last plea. I think I recognised the man at the same moment he recognised Jacques.

"The fire-eater," I said.

"Jacques… mon petit Jacques?" said Kamal. His voice was unsure – and much lighter than you'd expect from a man of his size – and he still held the club above him as if he hadn't yet decided whether to bring it down or not.

"Non, ce n'est pas vrai…"

"Oui, it's true, c'est moi, petit Jacques." He held his hands out to Kamal. I'd rolled away and was rubbing my neck.

"Owww," I moaned. Neither of them paid me any attention.

Kamal dropped his club and pulled Jacques to his feet. He squeezed Jacques so tight I feared he might turn him into raspberry jam. For what seemed an age neither of them moved (I don't think Jacques could have even if he'd wanted to). I could hear Jacques murmuring to Kamal but I made out only one word: Vette. I saw a thick tear somersault down Kamal's smooth cheek and onto Jacques' shirt.

I glanced up and down the track.

"Shouldn't we get back to the others?"

Chama and Chana were asleep when we returned.

"What in the name of..." began Pin as he caught sight of Kamal.

Chama opened his eyes. He looked up (and up) at Kamal and shook his head.

"See?" he said. "The Dragon Man. Told you." He closed his eyes again and appeared to have gone straight back to sleep.

On the walk back from the north wall Kamal had told us how he'd ended up in the fort. He spoke mostly in French and Jacques translated for me.

"He says he had no choice if he wanted to live, and what man doesn't want to live?"

Kamal grunted. He spoke English but only when he had to. He was wearing a pair of tatty trousers and sandals with nothing on his top half. His skin shone. Jacques said it was because of all the times he'd set himself on fire.

Kamal claimed to have been born in Constantinople but couldn't be absolutely certain about it. All he could be certain about was the circus. He couldn't remember a time when he wasn't in the ring.

It was not long after he'd led his circus away from Agra, muttering to himself about Jacques and Vette not being ready in time, that they'd been attacked. He was the only survivor – he set his cart on fire and sat inside it until the attackers went. Then, one by one as the sun beat down, he buried the magician, the horse riders, the juggler, the bird lady and finally the clowns and as he dug each grave and mourned his friends – his circus family – he realised how much he did not want to end up in the ground as well. No, he wanted to live.

Which was difficult because if the British saw him, with his dark skin, they would kill him and if the rebels saw him, an Ottoman, they would kill him. So when the deserters found him and, impressed by the ferocity with which he first fought them off, asked him to join them, he did. Because it offered a chance to stay alive.

"He asks me to forgive him, says he knows he's done wrong but it is hard to think when you have buried your people and just want to stay alive..."

"He's with them, the deserters?" I interrupted, as

a thought sprang into my mind. "George… does he know about George?"

I stepped in front of Kamal and put my hands out, as if ordering him to stop.

"Have you seen George?"

"Who is George?"

"My brother…"

"Your brother?"

"My brother."

His huge shoulders rose and fell. "I don't know your brother. What does he look like?"

"What does he look like, well… he's um… he's my brother and he's, he's… I don't know."

The last three words came out as a whisper. I don't know.

"The boy?"

"Yes, the boy – there's a boy being held hostage, we think in the fort." Jacques stepped in for me. I gave him a grateful smile, sniffed and asked the question I dreaded being answered.

"Is he all right… is George all right?"

Kamal reached out a meaty hand and rested it on my shoulder. "The little boy is thin because there is little food and he is scared I think, but he lives."

He gave my shoulder a quick squeeze. "I think he looks like you, his sister." A smile as wide as the ocean filled his face.

"That's why you are here? To free your brother George?"

I nodded. So did Jacques. The smile retreated.

"Then I shall help you."

As Chama and Chana slept on, the old man snoring gently, Kamal explained where George was being kept and how many of the deserters were on guard at any one time. He crouched down next to us and spoke in French, pausing while Jacques translated. He used his fingers to draw his own plan of the fort in the dust. When he was done he stood up and brushed his hands on his trousers. I noticed he had not a single line or mark on his palms.

"I must return or they will get suspicious – they are very jumpy, shoot at anything they see – every day somebody shoots at a monkey and shouts alarm. They're convinced the rani's coming for them – they murdered one of her messengers and presume she'll take her revenge. I'll come here early in the morning and you can tell me what I must do."

We all looked at Pin. He nodded. "I will have a plan by the morning."

And he did. Of course he did.

We spent the night up a tree, finding a broad branch, pulling off vines and fastening them around us so we wouldn't fall off while asleep. Chama and Chana slept on the ground, saying they were too old to climb trees. "Better," said Chama, "to keep our feet on the ground, it's where they should be."

It was the vines that helped Pin tie his plan together.

At first Jacques shook his head and said 'Non, non, it will never work.' Of course he did because he's Jacques. Yet this time even I wasn't convinced.

"They're too suspicious, they won't fall for it."

"They're frightened – didn't you hear what Kamal said? They're frightened and expecting bad things to happen," insisted Pin. "When you're frightened your mind plays tricks on you, you're scared by your own shadow."

"Dangerous," said Jacques. "Très, très dangerous."

"Blood and thunder," snorted Pin. "Dangerous… dangerous, says the boy who walks on air and flies like a bird, only he has no wings. Every step you take is dangerous."

"I cannot fly," said Jacques. But Jacques knew he would go along with Pin's plan.

"But, my dear friend, you are the Great Romanini, and you can fly… fly in and fly out. So we need a rope." Pin paused and held up a vine. "And here we have one."

"Aha," said Chama shaking his head. "Bind those together and you will have a rope stronger than anything man could make. Nature is stronger than man."

"Are you sure about this?" said Jacques. He wanted reassurance. "Absolutely sure?"

It was late afternoon and we were crouched on the edge of the forest again, watching the guards at the entrance. Chama and Chana had gone off to take their positions, where Pin would join them shortly.

"A storm is coming," Chama declared just before we separated.

"You can sense it Grandfather, in your bones?" said Pin.

"No, boy," said Chama, shaking his head. "Look in the sky, you can see it. Smell the air and you can smell it. A big storm." He followed Chana into the trees.

We sniffed. Chama was right – you could smell the coming rain. "It's perfect for the plan," announced

Pin, as if he'd known all along. "The mighty Indra has his hammer in his hand, he will help us beat those snakes."

"A hammer's not going to be much good against guns is it?" I suggested.

"No," said Pin, a note of irritation edging into his voice. "Indra is answering my prayers… our prayers, the god of storms, the slayer of serpents…"

"Pin? Are you sure about this?" Jacques interrupted to repeat his question.

"Yes," said Pin, his voice now definitely snappy.

A junglefowl squawked in the distance. I felt jumpy.

Jacques leaned towards me. "Imagine you're on the tightrope – think only of that, keeping your balance."

"I won't look down." I stood up.

"Ready?" said Pin. "You remember everything?"

Kamal nodded.

"Yes, Pingali." My voice had a kick to it. "Just because you're clever doesn't mean we're all stupid."

His face fell. "I'm just trying to help get your brother."

"I… I'm… oh, Pin, sorry – I'm a bit, a bit… scared."

I threw my arms around him.

"You are brave, Beatrice Spelling. Much braver than me – don't be scared of them."

"It's not them," I mumbled into his ear. "It's seeing George. What if I don't recognise him – what if he doesn't want me..."

"Nonsense," said Pin. "That is not in my plan at all. Ganesha will remove all obstacles between you and your brother."

I let go of him and smiled a thank you. His hands moved quickly and I looked down at my chest. His necklace hung there, the small elephant's head and human body. It felt weightless.

I shook my head. "No, Pin, no..."

"Yes," he said. "I believe in him so he will be with me always – you... well, now he is going with you as well."

"I... oh, Pin..."

He cut me off. "Remember the grandfather story... we never give up... never."

"Come," said Kamal. "Let us go."

The guards lifted their muskets when they saw us emerge from the cover of the forest. Kamal gave me a shove and I stumbled forward, only just managing to keep my balance.

"Stay on the tightrope," I whispered to myself.

"What you got there, Turk?" snarled one of the men as we drew closer.

Kamal placed a large hand on my shoulder and gripped hard. I let out a cry, as much of surprise as pain.

"Found her, hiding in the forest – says she's something to tell us."

"She looks English – she English?"

"I've come for my brother," I said, trying to keep my voice as firm as possible.

"She sounds sort of English," said the taller guard, who had a dark beard and long straggly hair that hung down to his shoulders. "More than you, Turk," added the other one and pushed out a guffaw through the gaps in his teeth to underline his point.

"I'll take her to the general," said Kamal, returning his hand to my shoulder. "Where is he?"

"Dunno," said the bearded one. "His room I guess. Shout him down."

We passed beneath the fort entrance and into the large cobbled courtyard. In front of us was a square building with a balcony running along the first floor.

Along one of the walls an animal pen held a couple of scrawny horses and three goats. In the middle of the courtyard a large stack of wood was piled high, ready to be lit for the night's bonfire. It was surrounded by chairs, benches and a couple of charpoys across which sprawled more men. Like the two guards outside they were dressed in a fraying mix of British army uniforms and Indian clothes plundered from villages, as if they'd been sent to pick an outfit from the dressing-up box in the attic and then fought over it.

"Woo-hooo," hooted one, leaping to his feet. "What have we here?"

As Kamal propelled me across the courtyard we were accompanied by a mini-mob of laughing, shouting men. One lent in and pinched me; Kamal swiped an arm at him. Another danced backwards in front of me pulling twisted faces.

"What we going to do with her?" yelled a squeaky voice.

"I'm taking her to see the general – no one shall lay a finger on her until the general has seen her." Kamal raised his voice so he might be heard above the tumult.

"Don't touch… don't touch… who do you think

you are, Turk?" A man almost – but not quite – the same size was standing in front of Kamal. He raised his hands and pushed at Kamal, who took a step back. I tripped and fell to the ground, my knee bashing against a broken cobble.

I gasped but no one heard me, no one paid any attention to me because they were all drawn to the two big men facing each other. We were surrounded now, me and Kamal, the men pressing around us, eyes bright at the thought of the coming fight. Kamal stepped over me and I clutched one of his legs. I'd fallen off the tightrope. I closed my eyes as the sounds of the men filled my ears.

A hand pulled at my leg, then another. They had hold of me and pulled. I clung on to Kamal's leg. I opened my eyes and found myself looking straight at the man who had killed Tonton. His eyes were yellow. I screamed.

He let go and tumbled backwards, landing on his back, pushing the rest of the men back from us.

"It's her..." he said, scrambling to his feet. I stayed where I was, clinging to Kamal's leg. He reached a hand down and pulled me to my feet. My head was spinning

"Her… she's, she's a…"

"What is she?"

A voice, barked from on high. The men all looked up. A small man with a white beard had emerged onto the balcony. He wore an immaculate British army uniform, an officer's uniform although one that seemed too big for him – the sleeves of the red coat were turned up and the golden epaulettes didn't have much shoulder to rest on. The tip of a shiny scabbard attached to his belt scraped along the balcony.

"General," began Kamal. "Found her in the forest, says she's a message for you – the rani's men, they're…"

"A witch," yelled Tonton's killer. "She's a witch. We can't have 'er here, we must kill 'er before she damns us all."

He reached out and grabbed my arm, pulled me in front of him. "She'll do for us if we don't do for 'er, General."

There were mutterings among the rest of the men.

"Nonsense," announced the general. "Bring her to me, Turk – we need to hear about the damn witch rani."

Tonton's killer held on to me. "Get your hands off me," I said and stamped on his foot.

"Aaarrrghh!" he yelped, trying to grab his foot, keep hold of me and his balance. He failed in all three and fell to the cobbles. "Witch…" He raised his voice and pointed at me. "She's a witch. I've seen it…"

"Cease your mad ramblings, Shaw," commanded the general. "You're not right in the head, man. Any more and I'll have you locked up. Now, bring the girl to me, Turk."

Kamal took my arm and set off for the building.

"Noooo!" yelled Shaw. "We must get her out – she commands the beasts…"

"Ignore him, he's a madman," whispered Kamal.

"I saw her command a tiger, a real tiger, it nearly killed me and it did for old Mick – it did what she said, I seen it with my own eyes, she set it on Mick. She'll bring the beasts of the forest down on us, tigers, elephants, monkeys even, a whole army of them."

There were murmurs around the rest of the men.

"Enough, Shaw," barked the general. "Enough."

The sky was darkening, but not yet with the night. The clouds were bringing Indra's storm. In the distance thunder rumbled, a growled warning of what was to come.

"See," yelled Shaw. "We must burn her."

"Aye," began someone else. "Witches have to be burnt, it's the only way, otherwise they come back to get you."

"Stuff and nonsense," said the general. "We're not in the dark ages." We moved inside the building, into a room that had once been grand, a throne on a raised platform at one end. The general reappeared and took his place on it. He beckoned Kamal towards him.

Kamal gave me another shove in the back. My breathing was short and sharp; I couldn't help it. This was not going as it was supposed to. Not at all.

"What's the girl's story, Turk?"

"Found her in the forest. She did not try to run away. Said she has important news for everyone in the fort."

"Well, girl?" The general turned to me, red coat, white beard, twinkly eyes. He looked quite mad. They all did. I gulped a mouthful of air.

"I know something, something that can save you, but I want something in exchange."

I stopped and stared at him, hard as I could, trying

to tell him I was not afraid, hoping he wouldn't notice that I was terrified of him and his men.

"Tell me what you want."

"You have George – he's my brother…"

"The boy, General, she means the boy."

"Quiet Turk, let her speak… you want the boy, what will you give me?"

"Information."

"What?"

"Bring my brother."

"What could a lost little girl possibly know that could help me – I am the general. People live or die on my command."

"I believe, sir, a good general succeeds because he knows more about his enemy than his enemy knows about him."

The general eyed me. "I am a great general."

"A great general would burn the witch."

I spun around. Several of the men had followed us into the room.

"Aye, burn her, General."

He waved a hand to quieten them. They fell silent. But for how long? This was no ordinary army where the soldiers followed every command.

"Tell me and you shall see your brother."

"And you will free us both?"

"You have my word." His eyes told me the truth, but it's what we expected. This could still work – if I kept my nerve (and if Pin and Jacques carried out their parts of the plan perfectly. Lots of ifs).

"The rani… her men – they're coming…"

"Nonsense, nobody knows we're here."

"The rani was told, a spy told her – she's sent scouts to investigate. They will be here tonight."

Another peel of thunder accompanied my words. It was louder, closer. The room was gloomy; then for a second it was brighter than any day.

"Lightning…" gasped one of the men.

"It's her… it's her, the witch – I told you." Shaw, Tonton's killer was back. "Burn her."

There were more men now crowded into the throne room. There was a murmur of agreement.

"Burn her, General," said one. "We must," said another. "At once," said a third.

They pressed forward. Kamal stood behind me, shielding me from them. More thunder.

"Burn herrrrr," snarled Shaw. *He* sounded like a witch.

"Burn her," agreed another, and another, and another.

The general looked over his men. He was losing control.

"Very well," he said. "Burn her."

The general drew his sword and waved it over his head. He raised his voice into a howl.

"Burn her and as she burns we'll fight the rani's rabble and kill every single one. No mercy, we'll bring fire and brimstone down on this accursed country. Death to all."

"Yarrrrgghhhh!" roared the men and pushed forward. Kamal was shoved aside and hands grabbed me. I lashed out. It was useless; my arms were pinned to my side and I was heaved upwards, carried above the pack of men.

I screamed; from the bottom of my being I screamed, and, as I did, there was another roll of thunder; then, almost at once, a crack of lightning.

"Burn the witch, burn the witch, burn the witch…" chanted the men.

"Kamal," I yelled. "KAMAL!"

"She's cursing us, quick get her on the fire."

We were back in the courtyard. I tried to kick and thrash my legs and arms but couldn't move them. I turned my head and caught sight of Kamal, a man behind him raising the butt of a gun above his head. I saw the butt fall and Kamal fall too.

"GEORGE!" I opened my mouth and let it out. "GEORGE!"

The second call received an answer, a cackle of gunfire followed by a yell from the gatehouse.

A guard appeared at the entrance, waving his gun. "They got Ernie, they're coming for us – the rani's here…"

There was another splutter of gunfire, followed by the whine of the bullets bouncing off the stone walls of the fort.

"TOOO ARRRRMMMSSS!" The general's voice boomed – a voice bigger than the man it came from – and was followed by the loudest roar of thunder yet. Darkness covered the sky; the day had been stolen. I could smell the storm, taste it. It filled my mouth as

I fell. The men dropped me and ran for the ramparts, shouting as they went.

Another clap of thunder, so much noise, from heaven and earth. More gunfire, more shouting, some screams.

The fall on to the cobbles knocked the breath from me. I shook my head. It wouldn't clear. I tried to get on to all fours. There was a hand around my ankle, hands around both ankles, strong hands, dragging me, my face against the cobbles.

I tried to twist myself to see who had me and where he was dragging me. I tried to wriggle and twist and thrash, like a fish desperate to get off the hook.

We reached the fire and he pulled me up. It was Shaw. "Witch," he hissed and spat in my face. "I will burn you."

He kicked my legs away and I collapsed to the ground again. He tied my arms around a large log, tied my feet. I couldn't stop him.

He disappeared. Not for long and, when he returned, he had a blazing torch in one hand. It threw light across his face and I could see how twisted it was. I don't think he was a man anymore. I don't know what he was, but I knew what he was going to do.

I pulled at the ropes and shouted at him, as if my anger could blow the torch out. I was not going to die like this, not when George was so close. Shaw grinned as he came closer, holding the torch out, ready to light the fire. I couldn't break free.

Thunder rumbled around the fort and a flash of lightning caught a surprised look on his face. There was a hand around his left ankle, a big hand.

"KAMAL!" I yelled.

He pulled hard and Shaw fell. Both tried to get to their feet. Kamal was groggy; I could see he was still feeling the effect of the blow to his head. The torch lay on the ground, its flames caressing the tinder-dry wood around me, tempting it to come alight. Shaw rose and reached for the torch; he just needed to flick it a little further and the fire would take hold.

I did nothing. There was nothing I could do but watch and see whether I was going to live or die.

Shaw reached the torch and lifted it, then curled back his arm ready to toss it on to the fire. The hand appeared again and seized hold of the torch. Shaw twisted around and saw Kamal rising over him, his hand clutching the torch, just where the flames began. Kamal wrenched the torch from Shaw's grip and fed the end into his own mouth – which opened like a python's wider and wider—and then the fire was gone.

With a roar, Kamal pulled the torch from his mouth, swung it round and clobbered Shaw on the head. He collapsed without a sound, like an unwanted ragdoll dropped from a child's hand.

"Kamal?"

He looked around, as if unsure where he was or what was happening. Clap after clap of thunder echoed across the fort, Indra's applause for Kamal's rescue act, and as it finished the rain began.

"Kamal… untie me… Kamal…"

His gaze fell to me. He grunted, pulled a knife from his belt and knelt behind me.

"Thank you," I said. My voice was hoarse from shouting. "You saved…"

"Quick," he said, his voice scratchy, "must find George. Petit Jacques will be on the way. He needs my help."

He hauled me to my feet and we set off for the building, crouching as we ran. The noise was ceaseless, thunder, gunfire, shouting, screaming, and the rain added to it, falling heavier and heavier, puddles already forming in the courtyard. The wind had picked up too, adding its howl to the night. It seemed as if every force of nature was being unleashed. Had we woken the dark spirits Chama said slept in the forest?

The deserters' attention was directed towards the forest. They were unleashing volley after volley into it, shooting blindly and shouting, shouting to try and check their fear of the dark and the storm and the strange events that had overtaken them.

And in reply there came a smattering of shots back from the forest. Pin and his sharpshooters, Chama and Chana, the three of them spread out and moving after each shot and making as much noise as they could. Their aim was not to kill anyone, just to confuse everyone.

I'd spent the afternoon teaching them to load and reload our three pistols while Jacques and Kamal built a succession of bonfires. Pin had lit them before they started shooting, just to add to the confusion. Beneath the rain, they were now billowing smoke.

We made the building, dripping wet footsteps across the throne room and then heading up. It grew hotter and hotter as we climbed the stairs to the top floor. Kamal hurried us down a long, dark corridor. At the far end he unbolted a small wooden door.

We entered a room barely lit by a small lamp flickering on a table. It was hot enough to sweat the devil. There was a tiny window at the far end, what little light it might have dragged in interrupted by bars lining the windowsill. Beneath the window was a charpoy. A hatch in the roof was propped half open by a long wooden pole.

"I must go and find Jacques – stay here," instructed Kamal. I nodded.

Beneath the hatch the rain had created a puddle on the floor. A figure knelt by it, small and thin beneath a tousled mop of hair. He – for I knew who it was – was scraping water off the floor, trying to catch some in the palm of his hand.

He sat back on his haunches and looked up at me.

"Hello, George," I said.

The boy scooped what little water he'd collected into his mouth and stood up. He stepped backwards. He had wide eyes and a dirty face. His copper-coloured hair pointed to every direction on the compass. His torn clothes were a match for his face.

"Who are you?"

His voice was faint. He took another step back.

"How d'you know my name?"

I stepped forward and put out a hand. Lord knows what I looked like to him, a wild jungle creature perhaps (but then I had only just escaped being burnt alive as a witch).

I opened my hand and showed him what I held.

He looked at Rabbit then up at me, his head

cocked to one side as he tried to work out what was going on.

He put out his hand.

"Are you… are you…"

I held my breath. I could feel my heart beating faster and faster. Tears pushed behind my eyes. I wanted to hold him, but he looked like a startled deer, ready to take flight if I made the slightest move.

I held Rabbit out for him. He was so small, so frail. "I made this for my brother – did you know that?"

He nodded and I took another step closer to him. He stayed still.

"Are you Beatrice?"

I nodded.

"Are you my sister?"

I nodded.

"Have you come to take me home?"

"We're going to find home, I promise."

He reached out and took Rabbit. I reached out and took him and he did not run away.

"Hello, wee brother," I said, just before a sob escaped. I swallowed, hard. This was no time to wobble. So instead I started to babble, like I do.

"Have you been to the circus, George? We could run away and join the circus if you like – I love the circus, you see I'm now an acrobat and I could teach you to become an acrobat with my friend Jacques, and my friend Pin can teach you instead of school because he's ever so clever. Or we could all go back to Glen Laddich and live with Grannie and look after Grannie... that would be a happy ending wouldn't it and children deserve to have happy endings, don't we?"

I wasn't looking for an answer. I squeezed him some more and held him as tight as I could.

"You'll like Pin and Jacques, they'll be your new brothers, your big brothers, we'll look after you..."

"Is it because I don't have a mother and father anymore?"

I let go of him and knelt in front of him.

"You've still got me, George – and I've still got you, and we must talk about Mother and Father whenever we can and I will tell you everything I remember about them and you must tell me everything you remember."

He nodded, chewing his lip as if unsure about this latest twist in his young life.

"We must go – Jacques is across." Kamal was back, waiting by the door.

"Is he a bad man?"

"No, George – Kamal saved my life and is helping save yours."

"Come," said Kamal and we reversed our steps out of the room and back down to the throne room.

Kamal led us behind the throne and out a smaller door into the back of the courtyard. Night had fallen. Rain was bouncing off the cobbles. The shooting continued out the front of the fort and the thunder and lightning still rumbled and fizzed above us. George pushed his hand into mine.

Kamal crossed first, kicked open the door to the dilapidated building and waved us over. We hared across the courtyard then up the steps to the top floor, into a room that matched George's prison, including the hatch in the roof.

"Have you got Rabbit?" I said. George nodded. "You must absolutely promise me you'll never leave it behind again."

He looked solemn. "I promise, Beatrice, cross my heart." He crossed his heart and looked up at me. I ruffled his hair.

"Right, now I'll tell you our plan – well, it's Pin's plan really."

Before I'd begun, the hatch opened and Jacques' face appeared. He lowered a rope.

"Quick," he said, "there's no time to lose."

"There never is," I muttered as I took the forest-made rope – vines coiled tightly together (while I'd spent the afternoon teaching shooting, Jacques had spent it rope-making) – and tied it beneath George's armpits.

Another rumble of thunder rolled across the sky.

"Come on, George, we're going on an adventure."

"Hurray!" cheered George.

"Shhh," I cautioned, "a secret adventure."

Jacques hauled him up to the roof. Kamal waved a farewell – hopefully a temporary one – he was to find his own way out because what we were about to do was not for a giant of a man.

CRRRAACCKKK.

More lightning forked across the sky and assaulted the earth, thrusting a bolt of light into the room. The rope dropped once more and I began to climb.

We were soaked through, all three of us. George reached out for me. I held his little hand tight, feeling the rain run down the back of my neck.

Another shaft of lightning speared across the fort. I saw where we had to go and shuddered. The homemade tightrope stretched into the darkness – our escape route put in place by Jacques and Kamal. If all went to plan we would vanish into the forest unseen by those fighting below. Jacques brushed his hair back off his forehead. He leaned close.

"Just like in the Big Top," he said and nudged me. The rain clattered against the roof like a drum roll.

I lifted George – he was light as a feather after being on prison rations for so long. Which was just as well – he would be easier for Jacques to carry.

"You've seen how the monkeys carry their babies when they swing through the trees, haven't you George?"

He whispered yes into my ear.

"We need you to be a baby monkey for Jacques – can you be a brave boy and do that?"

"Yes," he whispered, "I will for you, Beatrice."

"Let's go," said Jacques. He took off his shirt and I tied it around George and Jacques, binding them together. George squeezed his arms around Jacques' neck.

"Not so tight – I must breathe," said Jacques. "Ready little brother?"

"Yes," said George in a wobbly voice.

"Time to join the circus," said Jacques and stepped on to the rope. He stretched out his arms.

It's amazing, I thought, as I watched Jacques. He really could walk on air. They were swallowed by the night. Soon it would be my turn.

"I can walk on air," I said aloud. Maybe I was part-witch after all, maybe before I left home I'd been lent powers by the faerie folk Grannie said lived in the oak wood at the top of Glen Laddich. Or maybe it was because Ganesha was with me. I took a deep breath and stepped on to the rope. I extended my arms to help find my balance and set off into the dark.

It was a difficult crossing. It began badly and got worse, much worse. Kamal and Jacques had tied the rope tight but still the wind shook it and buffeted me.

It felt peculiar not to be able to see the ground out of the corner of my eye. On a "normal" rope walk a glimpse of the ground offers a reminder to maintain absolute concentration; otherwise that's where you will end up. And without a safety net that meant one thing: splat.

I fixed my eyes on an imaginary point in the darkness, picturing George's face beaming at me out of the night like a homing beacon, and stepped on across the gap between the building and the watchtower on the north wall. The steps up to it were unsafe so once across, we were safe. Once across…

Left and right, left and right, swinging my left leg out, then my right, feeling the rope beneath the hardened soles of my feet.

I was over halfway when it happened.

CRRAACCCKKK.

The lightning bolt zigzagged across the sky and hurtled into a tall tree just outside the fort walls. It was so close I swear I felt the heat of the bolt flashing past me. The tree burst into flames despite the rain still cascading down.

For a moment it was lighter than the brightest day.

"Oh no," I said and slipped.

My fall seemed to happen in slow motion. At least to start with. I felt it begin; my foot slid ever so slightly across the wet make-do tightrope and that's all that was needed. One tiny slip on the tightrope and it's the end. I began to flap my arms in a desperate attempt to keep my balance, perhaps even to try to fly away from my troubles.

If anyone had been watching, it would have happened in the blink of an eye, but for me it played out moment by frozen moment. My right foot began the fall. I whirled my arms as I felt my balance go; I was tipping backwards. I tried to lean forwards and felt my left foot go. For a split second, a click of the fingers, I was in mid-air; then I fell.

I thought I screamed but Jacques insisted it all happened without a sound – he heard nothing from the other side. So I must have screamed inside my head. Screamed an instruction to my left arm. I felt my body hit the rope and then it was scraping under my left armpit and along my left arm and then there would be nothing, nothing to touch until I slammed onto the cobbles below and that would be the end.

It was my left hand, or to be precise, the long fingers on my left hand, that saved me. I'm strong, as strong as any girl or boy; that's what comes of a childhood climbing trees, swimming in lochs and arm wrestling the laird's son (even if I thought he was a weakling). And my fingers and wrists were strong enough to stop me plunging straight to my death on that dark and stormy night in the old fort deep in the forest.

I felt the rope on my wrist, I felt it on my hand and I grabbed. Four fingers wrapped around the rope and broke my fall. The weight of my body tried to pull me off, wrenching my shoulder so painfully I feared it was dislocated. I let out a silent scream, and clung on.

I swayed in the wind, the rain running down my face, my neck, my back. My hair hung limply, damp, tangled and dirty, covering my eyes. Pain pulsed through my shoulder and along my arm. My strength felt as if it had already plummeted to the ground.

"Let go," something deep down inside instructed. "That's enough now… no more. Give up and let go, Beatrice. Let go, Beatrice. Let go."

The wind seemed to take up the tune. "Let go, Beatrice, let go." It whistled around my head.

I sighed; I had nothing left to give. Another bolt shot across the sky. And then it happened, in that second or so the courtyard was lit beneath me. At least I think it happened. I've never told anyone because I'm not sure I believe it myself. Not even Pin. Perhaps it was only meant for me. Perhaps I shouldn't tell.

There below in the courtyard, looking up at me was a figure, a figure with four arms, a large belly and an elephant's head. His trunk reached up towards me, one hand went to his belly and pulled at the snake around his middle. I remember how the tummy sagged a little as the snake came off and next, as darkness shrouded the courtyard again, I remember looking up and seeing the snake slithering along the tightrope, wrapping half

its body around the rope and the other half around my wrist, securing me to the rope.

I heard Pin's voice in my head… "Remember the great story… we never give up, never." I looked down but there was nothing to see. I clung on.

I don't know how long I hung there for, and I don't know how long the snake tied me to the tightrope and I don't know if there ever was a snake because when I looked up again it was just my fingers holding me. I felt the strength trickle back into my body. I wrapped my right hand around the small carving still hanging from my neck. Then I flung up my right arm. That made it eight fingers around the rope.

I began to sing to myself: Grannie's favourite song but with my own words, always my own words.

"O ye'll tak the high road an' I'll dangle oan the air road…"

I swung myself, once, twice, three times and on the third time got high enough to scoop my legs around the rope.

"And I'll be in Scotland afore ye…"

I couldn't let go – I had George to care for now. I couldn't leave George alone in the world, and I couldn't leave Jacques or Pin alone either. They had no one but me.

"On the bonnie, bonnie banks of Loch Laddich."

I hung on to the rope. I knew I didn't have long. I tipped my head back, trying to collect some rainwater in my mouth. So thirsty. My arms burning. Running out of time. I began to edge along the rope, feeling it scrape the skin on my legs; soon the skin was broken and I could feel a warm trickle of blood.

There was a noise below, men shouting. Had our escape been discovered already? One more flash of lightning and I would be plain to see, an easy target for their bullets. I had to get back on my feet; it was far quicker to walk across than pull myself over, and besides I didn't think I had enough strength left in my arms.

I pulled myself up, straining every muscle. I twisted on to the top of the rope – and found myself facing the wrong way, looking back the way I'd come. Should I stand up and try to turn around? I'd done it in Agra, back in the courtyard, and got pretty good at it. The difference was the difference between night and day; when I fell in the courtyard, and I did several times attempting this turn, I collected a smattering of bruises to arms, legs and pride. If I fell here, well, that was only going to end one way. So long, Bea...

I was struggling to clear my head, tiredness trying to condemn me to death. I blinked rapidly, blew a loose strand of hair away from my face and made a decision.

I hadn't the strength left to hang below the rope again, turn my hands, then heave myself back on top of the rope facing the right way. So I stood up, slowly straightening my legs, arms outstretched but perfectly still.

I breathed out as I stood up; the rope felt good beneath my feet. Like they belonged together. I would not fall again. The feeling surged through my body, along my arms, down through my legs and into my toes. Quickly I raised myself on to the ball of my left foot and pirouetted, my right leg swinging round, searching for the comforting feel of the rope.

It was done in a flash; I swayed and my arms flapped a little and then I was upright and still. I took a deep breath and walked on, exactly as Jacques had taught me in the courtyard.

It seemed to me, as I approached the watchtower

on the north wall, that I had given my greatest-ever performance and not a single soul had witnessed it. Well, perhaps one had.

The turret and wall loomed out of the darkness and there they were, Jacques and George. Soon I was close enough to see the smiles on their faces. George leapt up and down and clapped his hands, Jacques put a gentle hand on his shoulder to calm him down. I leapt from the rope and into Jacques' outstretched arms.

One more descent. Then we could rest. I wasn't sure what I had left. Jacques, after cutting the tightrope, began to lower his other rope slowly over the vines, down towards the forest.

"I'll go down first with the boy on my back again – you follow, stay on our rope, it's too dark to try and use the other vines."

George leapt on. He enjoyed being given a piggyback by his new big brother, especially when they were doing something fun like clambering down a rope.

I watched the two heads disappear beneath me and waited, giving the rope an occasional tug to see if they had reached the bottom. When it felt clear, I gave one last look around and with the coast clear clambered over the battlements and began my descent.

Jacques had warned me not to try and slide because the roughness of the vine rope would rip my hands to pieces. The rope was beginning to fray near the top so I didn't hang around. My arms were aching again by the time I reached the bottom of the rope, which ran out the height of a man short of the ground. Jacques reached up to catch me as I let go and we collapsed to the ground. As I hit the forest floor the last of my strength dribbled from me, like Samson after Delilah cut his hair.

George was standing over me, hopping from foot to foot in excitement. "The rope ran out and Jacques said we had to jump and we jumped and landed in a heap and I was hurt but Jacques said I was as brave as the bravest soldier because I didn't cry. I didn't cry, Beatrice, I didn't cry... Beatrice? Are you... are you crying? Have you hurt yourself?"

I hadn't but I was crying, tears washing paths down my dirt-covered face. The dam burst deep within and I covered my face with my hands.

"Beatrice?" George sniffed and wiped his nose on his sleeve, confused by the sudden change in me.

"Here," said Jacques, reaching out his hand. "She'll catch us up, she just needs a little Bea time."

George took the older boy's hand and followed him into the trees. "What's Bea time?"

I let out another sob; it shoved its way out, hurting my chest. I pressed my palms against my eyes, trying to stop the tears.

"Enough," I said. "What would Miss Goodenough say?"

I giggled at the thought, a snotty giggle.

"Beatrice Spelling stop that sniffling at once and pay attention. You're still in a tight spot, young lady."

I sniffed and rubbed my eyes. I expect there will be sadness in me for a long time, perhaps forever, stored in a corner, quiet for much of the time but not all the time. Because I am an orphan. Not that different to Pin and Jacques. I should ask them about it – perhaps they are the same. Perhaps I shouldn't try and keep everything locked inside me. And George – I had to see George safe first and then I could cry.

I stood up and brushed what muck I could from my legs. Once more I put on my best Miss Goodenough voice, although to be honest it did shake a little as I spoke: "What a state Miss Spelling, an absolute state." I hurried after Jacques and my dear wee brother.

We spent what remained of that night and the next handful of days living like monkeys in the trees while we waited for Pin and Kamal, hoping they too had escaped. Pin was to help Chama and Chana home first, so they were safely out of the way before coming to find us. Kamal, well, we didn't know what Kamal would do, but we knew what he'd done. I'll never forget what Kamal did for me and George.

In the forest we found a tall, leafy tree not far off the track to the fort and climbed up into its broad branches. Before we climbed, I arranged a small pile of stones on the edge of the track while Jacques carved a mark into the tree's trunk: TT. It stood for Tonton – our tiger was to forever be our password – and, along with the pile of stones, it would tell Pin where we were waiting for him.

Twice we heard men pass on the road, the murmur of voices and clink of weapons. The coming of the rains brought the forest to life, turning it from brown to green, a sudden explosion of life and vegetation. The leaves of the great tree hid us.

It also gave shelter from the daily downpours,

when it sounded like we were sitting in the middle of the percussion section of the world's largest orchestra as the rain beat a relentless rhythm on the forest's canopy.

There wasn't much to do – after all we were hiding out in a forest. One afternoon George and I sat in silence watching a colony of ants on the march, a thin red line that would let nothing stop its progress. Some even carried small leaves or twigs which made it look as if the forest floor itself was on the move.

I tried to think of games to occupy George. One afternoon he suggested I spy.

"S," he began.

"Sky?" I suggested. He shook his head.

"Sun?" Another shake.

"Snake?" I said, looking around just in case.

"No."

"Er…"

"D'you give up?"

"Yes."

"Sister – S for my sister."

I hugged him tight. I couldn't stop hugging him.

"Get off, Beatrice, off me…"

There wasn't much to eat. Our stomachs rumbled

a good deal but we were not yet desperate enough to try to eat insects. We picked fruit and later found a mahua tree with its large fleshy flowers that were surprisingly good. It was Jacques who found it – with the help of a sloth bear. Pin had told him about the bears, harmless unless threatened. Jacques remembered Pin telling him how humans and bears who live in the great forests like nothing better than the taste of a mahua flower.

One morning Jacques saw a bear pass beneath the tree, a baby hanging on its back. "Like you George," he said and nudged the boy. They were clumsy animals, lumbering noisily around the undergrowth like they couldn't quite remember what they were supposed to be doing and where they were supposed to be doing it; a far cry from the ferocious bears that hunted in my storybooks at home.

Jacques dropped down from the tree and followed. He returned an hour later with an armful of mahua flowers. At first George took a bit of convincing to try a bite, only to then eat so many he made himself sick and spent the rest of the afternoon lying on the broadest branch, groaning.

Pin arrived that evening. George had stopped

groaning and fallen asleep. Jacques too was sleeping. I was walking on my hands along a branch above them.

"Oh hello – you're upside down," I said when I saw him peering at the tree trunk, running a hand over the scratched TT. Pin jumped. "Got you!" I said and swung down onto the broad sleeping branch.

"Come on up."

Before we woke the others I slipped Pin's necklace over my head and hung it back in its rightful place. "Thank you," I said.

We sat in the tree – Pin handing out chapattis Chana had made for his journey – and he filled us in. Chana and Chama were safe and Pin had seen nothing of the deserters. The three of them had kept shooting into the night until they felt we'd had time enough to escape, then slipped away into the forest.

When we were finished Pin passed around a bag of Chana's special honey sweets and we sucked on them as if tasting the nectar of the gods.

"Are we going to live in the tree forever?" wondered George, breaking the silence.

Pin shook his head. "I have a…"

"Plan." Jacques and I finished his sentence for him.

"So do I," said Jacques.

"Share it then," I said, taking the last sweet, licking it then sticking it to the branch – for Ganesha. "Just so long as it means we'll be together… forever and ever."

Epilogue – three years later

The man pushed past without even an excuse-me. Mrs Smith tutted and straightened her hat. She shook her head as well. This really was the most manner-less place, not at all like India.

She sighed when she thought back to Agra. She'd been happy there, in the beginning. A boy dashed towards her and dodged out of her way at the last second. Mrs Smith tutted again, or rather let out half a tut before she caught herself and cut it short.

She was doing a lot of tutting of late. Nothing pleased her. She sighed and shook her head. That too, sighing and headshaking. She disliked herself for it. What had happened to the young woman who'd sailed from England in search of adventure to last a lifetime?

There had been a chance once, for adventure. But she'd not taken it and she regretted it every day.

"Tut," she said, catching sight of a puddle collected in the broken pavement. This was not a part of the town they usually came to, but for one night only… she was looking forward to it.

"This way, my dear, careful now."

She looked round at the man who held her arm. Mr Smith, her husband of 13 and a half months. Perhaps it was the name. The name was turning her into a Mrs Smith, an empire wife who had nothing better to do than tut and tsk at the locals.

She'd had such a nice name before, an interesting name, and she'd had something interesting to do with her days. It had been enough for her. At least she thought it had. No one else around her did.

"You'll be left on the shelf," they said, ignoring the fact she was happy on her shelf.

Along came Mr Smith the banker, the terribly rich banker, the money man from Singapore, who was looking for a wife.

"You can't stay a schoolmistress all your life, that's not good enough for you, my dear."

She wished she was still Goodenough. She'd liked

being Miss Goodenough. She glanced out of the corner of her eye at Mr Smith, as if worried he might be able to read her thoughts. She felt guilty; he was a good man, good enough for her, she supposed. She reached out for his hand and tried to squeeze it. He pulled it away.

The look he directed at her – he was a man of few words – said, "What on earth are you doing?" Mr Smith didn't believe in public shows of affection. "Not the done thing, not the done thing at all. Tsk, tsk."

She sighed; at least they had the circus to look forward to, a travelling circus all the way from France here in Singapore; who would have thought it? She hadn't been to a circus since, let's see, Agra, of course… since Agra. The awfulness that followed that night in the Big Top had made her quite forget about it. She'd wanted to leave India after that.

Perhaps that was why she'd leapt at Mr Smith's offer of marriage. She'd been convalescing in the islands, a soothing holiday after the siege to settle her nerves. Mr Smith, Henry, had seemed taller and more charming under the palm trees.

Above the houses she could see the circus flag, positioned on the Big Top, fluttering a welcome. The crowds heading in its direction quickened their pace at first glimpse. Because everyone, young and old, wants to go to the circus.

At the entrance stood the ringmaster, dressed in an immaculate red tunic with gold epaulettes and gold stripes down each leg of blue trousers that disappeared inside well-polished leather boots. On his head he wore a turban so white it shone; a large purple jewel pinned to its front sparkled. Around his neck a small, wood-carved elephant's head dangled on the end of a chain.

"Roll up, roll up," he bellowed. "Welcome to the magic world of the circus, a world where anything can be." He was young, Mrs Smith thought. "You are to be served a tiffin treat this evening my lords, ladies and gentlemen, a treat so sweet it would please the great Ganesha… the greatest show on earth."

He twirled his baton, threw it heavenwards and caught it in one raised hand. In the other hand, Mrs Smith saw, he clutched a book. How odd, she thought.

"Madame," he said, catching Mrs Smith's eye. "Ask me a question, any question."

Mrs Smith looked alarmed. "I beg your pardon?"

"Je suis the amazing memory man – a walking

encyclopaedia – I remember everything. Every verse of the greatest story ever told. Tout le monde…"

Mr Smith had heard enough. "How dare you address my wife – I will not have a native speak to my wife in such a manner."

"Ah," said the ringmaster. "I may, sir, be brown on the outside but cut me open and my heart beats just the same as yours."

"Why you…" cried Mr Smith and raised his white-gloved hand just as the first act, the horses, dashed into the ring. The crowd surged and carried the Smiths beneath the Top and almost into their seats.

The evening passed quickly, a string of acts, riders, magicians, clowns, came and went, all introduced by the young ringmaster, who also took questions thrown at him from the packed stands – and answered them all.

Then came the fire-eater, a colossus of a man from his cannon-ball head, shining beneath the gaslights, down to his smooth-skinned torso and legs like tree trunks. His assistant, a young boy with copper-coloured hair, lit great flaming torches and the man – Mrs Smith didn't quite catch his name but it was something like camel – gulped them down. For his finale he set his arms alight and turned a flaming cartwheel to roars from the crowd, or most of the crowd.

Mrs Smith sighed. She could feel Mr Smith sitting bolt upright next to her. He wasn't enjoying the show so would be in a grump when they returned home.

"Nooooowwww, the one you've been waiting for, all the way from beautiful Pareee the greatest act in the history of the circus… the airwalkers… laddddieess and gentlemen I give you… no, they need no introduction…"

A young man and woman ran into the ring, holding hands. They stopped in the middle and bowed, spun around and bowed again. They wore matching purple outfits with a leaping tiger motif stitched on the back of their shirts. The woman had a green and gold silk scarf knotted around her waist.

They took a rope each and climbed swiftly and with great grace to the top of the Top. Mrs Smith tipped her head back to watch. And kept it tipped back throughout the display that followed.

The crowd ooohhh'd and aaaahhh'd and Mrs Smith ooohhh'd and aaaahhh'd with them, ignoring the furious glances from Mr Smith, who cleared his throat to add to his point.

When it looked as if the woman was about to fall, wobbling on the rope and dropping off only to fling out a hand and catch the rope in the nick of time, Mrs Smith flung a hand over her mouth to stifle a screech.

When the acrobats were done, swinging down off the safety net and landing neatly back on the hard, dusty floor of the ring, Mrs Smith joined the standing ovation.

"Oh Henry," she said, looking down at him as he clapped his still-gloved hands together with more gusto than she'd ever seen him do anything, "weren't they simply wonderful. Quite took my breath away."

Mr Smith couldn't help himself. He smiled at her and stood up. "Yes, my dear, weren't they… bravo!" he cried before remembering who he was supposed to be and sitting down.

That was the finale and the rest of the circus, led by the ringmaster, joined the acrobats in the ring.

"All for one and one for all," yelled the ringmaster as he led the bows. "And never forget ladies and gentlemen, the show…"

"MUST GO ON!" roared the rest of the circus as one.

The acrobats took a final bow of their own together and then a boy, the fire-eater's assistant, pushed between them and took a hand of theirs in each of his. They began to walk the ring, waving at the crowd. There was something familiar…

"Come along, my dear, enough of this now," said Mr Smith, striding off up the aisle at his brisk gentleman's pace.

Mrs Smith took a couple of steps after him before pausing for one last look back. The acrobats and the boy were near her on their farewell lap of honour, just an easy leap away. The woman – no, she was younger, still a girl really – caught her eye. She was tall and gangly, all arms and legs and a great big smile beneath bright green eyes, a mound of bronze-red hair piled on her head and somehow held in place.

Mrs Smith froze, her mouth dropped open.

"Beatrice," she said. "Beatrice Spelling?"

Mrs Smith started back down the aisle. The acrobats moved away, hurried on by the clowns, one of whom was wearing an enormous elephant mask. She hadn't noticed that before. The boy danced happily among them, lifting his arm and waving it in front of his face as if it were his own trunk.

The girl glanced back.

"Come along, Georgie," she said and put her hand out for the boy.

"Beatrice Spelling," said Mrs Smith again, louder.

The girl looked back once more. She grinned at Mrs Smith and for the rest of her long life Mrs Smith considered it the happiest smile she'd ever seen.

THE END

Q&A with Robin

Why did you decide to write a story set in this time, India in 1857?

For years two large folders have sat beneath my desk, gathering dust and then being chewed by my daughters' rabbit. I had to move them out of the rabbit's reach to save them and while doing so opened one and began reading…

Inside were copies of a Victorian-era diary written by my great-great grandad. James Scott-Elliot worked for the British East India Company, the body that by the middle of the 19th century effectively ruled much of India, having tricked, traded and forced its way into a position of immense power.

Having lost his job in Britain and seen his family fall on hard times, a young James needed work and a family friend found him a position in Calcutta (now Kolkata). On the long voyage down and around Africa and across the Indian Ocean, James sees whales, albatrosses and dolphins – one day his ship collides with a whale, on another a crewman is lost overboard, on another they discover a stowaway. In between James writes poems and performs in plays put on by the ship's passengers. Once in Calcutta he settles into his new job and the diaries record the life of a Briton in 19th century India, day-to-day details, flower shows, the hot weather, the wet weather, homesickness and gossip dotted with occasional more dramatic happenings, a servant is killed by a snake, a friend is mauled to death by a tiger during a hunt

Then comes 1857 and the rebellion and James writes of 'oceans of blood'. It was an extraordinary, dangerous and frightening time for all those involved and children were caught in the middle of it. Reading James' diary made me want to learn more of India and the rebellion in particular. The more I read, the more I wanted to set a story in this time, a time many of us in the UK know very little about.

But about who and what exactly should my story be?

What settled it was a single line I came across in a history book. I got lucky. Among those caught in the siege of Agra, recorded the historian Christopher Hibbert, was a French travelling circus. It was just an aside, but it leapt off the page. I read it again and again – a circus stuck in a siege! This was too good to be true. Everyone loves a story about the circus!

Next I found an old list of the Europeans – as non-Indians were known – trapped in Agra during the siege, among them 20 French nuns, led by Madame St Bruno, and a Romanini and Mademoiselle Santine, as well as a teacher called Miss Goodenough and other names I use in the Acrobats – they are all taken from history or James's diary.

The story I have written, following Bea, Ali and Jacques on their adventure, is of course fiction but what goes on around them is based on real events.

James Scott-Elliot, by the way, lived in Calcutta for 24 years before returning to Scotland. He was followed to India by five brothers and sisters, two of whom died there. My family's connection with India didn't end there; my great uncle, Charlie Anderson, fought and died alongside Indian soldiers as part of the Sirhind Brigade in the trenches of the First World War.

So what was the Indian Rebellion of 1857?

It began in Meerut when 85 Hindu and Muslim soldiers were sentenced to 10 years hard labour by the British for refusing to use new bullets for their rifles. These bullets came in wrapping that had to be ripped open by hand or teeth and it was claimed they were greased with cow and pig fat – which meant according to their religion Hindus and Muslims couldn't touch them.

The rumour spread like wildfire around the East India Company's army. Most of the soldiers were Indian but with British officers. At the time there were around 100,000 Britons, soldiers and civilians, ruling over 250 million Indians.

Over the previous two centuries the East India Company had grown from a trading company into a vast organisation that in effect ruled huge areas of India. By 1857 there was mounting anger with the Company among Indian soldiers, landowners and peasants. A wide variety of issues came together to make the country ripe for rebellion and it was the soldiers in Meerut who started it off.

In India it is often called the First War of Independence, while other historians call it an uprising or a rebellion. For many Indians it is seen as the beginning of their long struggle for independence.

The rebellion quickly spread across northern and central India with landowners and peasants joining in. The year-long conflict was brutal and bloody. Many more Indians were killed than Britons. The British response was extreme and barbaric. Anyone with links to the rebellion was executed, as well as many innocent people, villages were burned and the British even destroyed much of the beautiful ancient city of Delhi.

Afterwards the East India Company was shut down and the British government took over direct rule of India. It was not until 1947 that India at last became an independent country.

What happened to the Rani?

The Rani was queen of Jhansi, a state in northern India. She took power when her husband died, despite opposition from the British. Believed to have been born in 1827, Manakarnika, as she was first called, learnt to read and write, ride, use a sword, wrestle and weightlift when she was a teenager, all skills that women of the time were largely not allowed to do. In 1842 she married the Maharaja of Jhansi, changing her name to Laxmibai or Lakshmi. And she continued to do things her way – she wore a turban, which was seen as a man's dress, and taught other women to ride. After her husband died in 1853 the East India Company tried to get her to hand over Jhansi to them. "Meri Jhansi nahin dungee," she is supposed to have said. "I will not give up my Jhansi."

Exactly why the Rani sided with the rebels in 1858 is uncertain – there are different versions – but when the British sent an army to capture Jhansi she led the resistance.

Her army was beaten and she escaped on her horse with her son tied to her back. She joined other rebels in Gwailor and continued the fight against the British, leading attacks on horseback with her maids alongside her. In June 1858 she was killed in battle.

Today there are numerous statues to her in India, where she is seen as one of the country's first independence fighters.

It is not only on the Indian side that people were entranced by the Rani. The British too were in awe of her. One British soldier, John Latimer, said: "Her courage stands pre-eminent and can only be equalled but not eclipsed by Joan of Arc."

She sounds an incredible woman, a true hero on so many levels. One of my favourite things about writing stories set in history is what I find out on the way. I get taken to places I never expected to go and learn things I'd never expected to learn. I'd never heard of the Rani of Jhansi but following this history trail to India has helped me learn about her and her country.

She sounds an incredible woman, a hero on so many levels.

Was there really a travelling circus in the siege of Agra?

Yes – and with a Romanini and Mademoiselle Santine among them. What happened to them and the rest of the circus after the siege is unrecorded.

The second half of the 19th century was a boom time for the circus. In Paris nightly crowds of 15,000 would squeeze in to catch the acrobats, snake charmers, clowns, strong women, magicians, jugglers and all the rest. A family of leading acrobats could earn up to 4,000 francs, an excellent living for the time. Circus performers would study Der Artist, their own newspaper which would list jobs for acrobats, lion tamers, clowns etc. Can you imagine what an advert might look like: Wanted one lion tamer, no previous experience required…

European circuses travelled to India, and all around the world. There were tours to South America, Mexico, Cuba, Japan, Singapore and China as well as India. Some would then recruit local performers and take them back to Europe, one French circus went to China in 1854 and brought home a troupe of Chinese acrobats who introduced European audiences to plate spinning. PT Barnum, of Greatest Showman fame, was making his name in America at this time.

One last question… Pingali never did tell Bea his story about Ganesha – how did he come to have an elephant head?

There are several versions of how Ganesha got his head. This is my favourite: his mother, the goddess Parvati, moulded Ganesha from clay or the turmeric paste she used to bathe with. Parvati then set him to guard the door while she had a bath because her husband, the great god Shiva, had a habit of barging in while she was washing and she wanted to be left in peace. Shiva returned home unexpectedly and found Ganesha barring his way. The furious Shiva set his demons on the boy but Ganesha defeated them. Shiva stepped in and fought Ganesha, a battle that ended with the boy being beheaded (some versions have his soldiers or followers doing the beheading). Now it was Parvati's turn to be furious and she demanded Shiva bring their son back. Shiva sent his men out to find a new head, they returned with the head of an elephant and so Ganesha was restored to life.

Ganesha is the Hindu god of beginnings, regarded as the remover of obstacles so before setting out on a journey, like Pin, Bea and Jacques, you can call on Ganesha's help. He is also, by the way, the god of writers. And he does like sweets. A lot.

Robin Scott-Elliot has been a sports journalist for 25 years with the BBC, ITV, Sunday Times, Independent and the 'i', covering every sport you can think of and a few you probably can't. In 2012 he covered the London Paralympics as the Independent's Paralympic Correspondent. He threw that all away to move home to Scotland and write. He lives on the west coast with his wife and two children. His first book for children, *The Tzar's Curious Runaways,* was published in 2019.

Praise for *The Tzar's Curious Runaways* by Robin Scott-Elliot

'A brilliantly suspenseful novel, which should have even the most reluctant reader eager to reach the next cliff-edge.'
The Telegraph, the Best Children's Books of 2019

'A magical tale that immediately scoops up the unsuspecting reader to propel them on a breath-catching journey across snow-capped Russia. A thrilling and thought-provoking page-turner, effectively fusing historical fact with magic, mystical maps, wizards and wood spirits.
The Book Trust

'A vividly told debut.'
Fiona Noble, The Bookseller, October previews

'A magical, heart warming and gripping adventure novel.'
The Scotsman

'Historical fiction at its best.' The Reading Zone

'From fighting with wolves to an intense getaway across an icy river, Scott-Elliot skilfully describes the action in a way that keeps readers glued to the page.' Scottish Book Trust

'A truly enchanting and exceptional début with all the callings of a contemporary classic. Storytelling magic.'
Scott Evans, The Reader Teacher

'A vivid and vibrant adventure celebrating difference and friendship. Thrilling and moving.' Clare Balding

'A wonderful blend of factual research and magical adventure.'
Just Imagine

'A gripping and suspenseful story.' Get Kids into Books

'A beautifully crafted debut brimming with adventure – a classic in the making.' A. M. Howell, author of The Garden of Lost Secrets